Acclaim fo

Catell's voice was matter of fact. "Who are the two guys just came in the door?"

Paar turned and glanced toward the entrance. "They come quite often. Local detectives."

Catell rose slowly. He put his hands in his pockets, turned his back to the cops, and looked casual. "Hear this, Paar. Keep them and anybody else you know out of my way. If you don't, I'll get you."

Then he walked away, slowly, without turning. He went through an empty kitchen, then down a long hall. He picked a door, opened it, and found himself in a small cubicle without windows. A naked light bulb made a hard light, and under it stood Lily.

She had taken her shoes and stockings off and her hands were at her back, trying to undo the black corset. Catell closed the door behind him and she looked up.

"Fancy meeting you here, Lily." She didn't answer. Only her eyes moved. "If you were going to scream, don't," Catell said. He turned the catch of the door. "I'm just staying a minute."

She looked at him, frowning, and put a hand to her breasts. "Please," she said. "Please leave."

Catell heard footsteps in the hall and leaned lightly against the door, both hands on the knob. "Not a word, kid."

"Please, mister, I—"

Catell moved across the small room fast and clapped one hand over her mouth, holding her up against him with his other arm. He didn't have to say any more. She saw his face grow stiff, mean, and she stayed very still...

STOP
THIS MAN!

by **Peter Rabe**

A HARD CASE CRIME NOVEL

A HARD CASE CRIME BOOK
(HCC-058)
August 2009

Published by

Dorchester Publishing Co., Inc.
200 Madison Avenue
New York, NY 10016

in collaboration with Winterfall LLC

*This book is a work of fiction. Names, characters, places, and
incidents either are the products of the author's imagination or
are used fictitiously, and any resemblance to actual events or
persons, living or dead, is entirely coincidental.*

ISBN 0-8439-6120-1
ISBN-13 978-0-8439-6120-1

Cover design by Cooley Design Lab

Typeset by Swordsmith Productions

Printed in the United States of America

Visit us on the web at www.HardCaseCrime.com

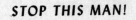

STOP THIS MAN!

Chapter One

Twenty-four Chester Street was a rooming house. Every morning at eight, weather permitting, the old woman from Room 4 stepped out on the porch, dragged a wicker chair to the railing, and sat.

This one morning she didn't show until eight-thirty. She stood for a moment wheezing the fine spring air into her lungs and patting her frizzy hair. Then she patted her cheek, doing it gently, as if the bright color of her face gave her pain. She dragged the wicker chair to the railing and sat.

The old woman had a trick she did with her upper lip, curling it back and giving a frightful view of her false teeth. That happened every few minutes, like clockwork, except this time. She suddenly got up from her chair, not quite fast enough, and vomited.

At a quarter to nine the two girls from Room 11 found her there on the porch. The old woman started to twitch a little when they dragged her back into the house, and by the time they had her under the light that hung by the staircase she was struggling to get free.

"Lemme go, for heaven's sake, lemme—"

"Mrs. Tucker, you fainted. Lie still now, Mrs. Tucker."

"Get your hands offen me, you! I never been sick a day in my life. Get your hands offen me," and she started to screech the way she always did.

They left her sitting on the stairs, under the twenty-five watt bulb, because they had to be at work ten minutes later.

Mrs. Tucker tried to get up but another retch tightened her insides and she doubled over. When the spasm had passed, she looked up. The landlady stood there, a big shape wrapped in a pink housecoat that was meant for a much more beautiful woman.

"You sick or something?" said the landlady. "You trying to mess up my front hall?"

"I never been sick a day in my life," and the old woman tried to get up.

That's when she fainted the second time.

With a fat man's grunt Dr. Junta hauled himself up the porch steps. He eyed the woman in the pink wrapper who was sloshing water over the planks of the porch and said, "I'm the doctor. Did somebody—"

"Number Four. End of the corridor on the left. And if she got something catchy," the landlady yelled after him, "get her out of here."

Number 4 was right next to Number 5; in fact, the two rooms had been one. There was a dividing wall, beaverboard on one side and the bare studding showing on the other, where the old woman had her bed.

"I don't want no doctor," she said when Junta came in. "I never been sick a day in my life and I didn't call for you."

"I understand you fainted." Dr. Junta put his satchel down.

"You got no call comin' in here like that. I didn't ask for you and I don't want you."

"If you're worried about the money, I'm from the Relief Board. Now, what happened? You threw up?"

The old woman did the trick with her teeth and gave Dr. Junta a cold stare.

"Indigestion is all. I know how to take care of myself."

"When did it start?"

"Just this morning. I'm all right now, so there's no need to hang around."

Dr. Junta sighed and opened his satchel. He wasn't a very enthusiastic man, but there were certain routine things that he always did. He shook down the thermometer and walked up to the bed. That's when he noticed the color of the woman's face.

"Where'd you get that sunburn this time of year?"

"I ain't got no sunburn. Where would I get a sunburn, anyways, holed up in this rat trap?"

"If you don't like the place," the landlady said from the door, "you can git any time, Mrs. Tucker. Any time!"

"All right, both of you," said Dr. Junta. "Now, once more, Mrs. Tucker, try to remember how you've felt the last few days. Any complaints, any discomforts."

"Nothing. I been fine."

"She been fine like a sick dog," said the landlady. "Sickish for days, borrowing my aspirin and lying in that bed of hers."

"She's wrong. Listen, Doctor—"

"How long has this been going on?" asked Dr. Junta.

"Lemme see now." The landlady rewrapped herself and looked up at the ceiling. "Right after that one-nighter was here. Smith, he said his name was. Middle-aged guy, real pale face, wore a blue overcoat. Right next door, he stayed, in Number Five."

"Was his bed behind this wall here?" Dr. Junta tapped on the thin partition.

"No. That's where the closet is."

"Was Smith sick, as far as you could tell?"

Smith, the pale man in the blue overcoat, hadn't been sick as far as any of them knew, but the hot, sore color of Mrs. Tucker's face wasn't a simple rash, as the old woman was trying to say, and Dr. Junta couldn't decide just what it might mean. That night, playing it safe, he committed Mrs. Tucker to the Hamilton City Hospital.

Jack Herron threw his cigarette on the floor and stepped on it. Then he picked it up and put it in the ashtray on his desk. He looked at his watch, then at the phone next to his elbow. He had been doing this all day, but nothing had happened. No news.

Stiff from sitting, Herron walked up to the dark window and looked at his reflection in the glass. He looked properly nondescript. An FBI man looks like anybody else and makes an effort to stay that way. He patted his thin hair into place self-consciously, wishing the early balding didn't show so much.

Herron smoked another cigarette and then he couldn't stand the waiting any longer. He grabbed his hat off the hook, clicked the safety lock, and slammed the door behind him. Lettering on the door said, "Federal Bureau of Investigation, District Office, St. Louis, Mo."

A few blocks from the office Herron turned up a broad flight of stairs and walked into the Central Police Station. Maybe something had come through since he left the office.

There was a little room right off Communications smelling of varnish and sweeping compound. Herron walked in and said hello to the two men at the table. They were sitting in shirtsleeves and the older of the two was pouring black coffee into paper cups. The young one was wearing a shoulder holster.

"Hello, yourself," said the one with the holster. "If you want coffee, we got. If you want news, we ain't got."

The old one who worked in the next room put a cup before Herron and poured from a tin percolator. "I know what he wants," said the old one, "but he's going to get coffee."

Herron sat down, sipped from his cup, and said, "That's too bad, Starkey."

"He don't like your coffee," said the young cop who was wearing the shoulder holster. "He thinks it's just too bad for words. Myself, I drink Starkey's coffee because I like the flavor of the paper cups. Eh, Starkey?"

"Shuddup," said Starkey.

Herron knew there was no point in asking whether anything had come through. Starkey would have told him.

"Listen, Herron," Starkey said. "Why all this mummery with a message? If it's got to be coded, why don't you guys receive it yourselves? Why have us receive it?"

"That's because the FBI is federal," said the young cop. "They do things different. They have the local police receive their messages so the police can phone it in and waste a little time getting it through. It's more complicated that way."

Starkey laughed, but Jack Herron didn't think it was so funny.

"First of all, the message isn't coded. Secondly, we got no night operator. And why aren't you watching your ticker?"

"I got Jones watching," Starkey said. "And Jones knows as much about it as I do: 'Upon receipt of the following convey immediately to local office Federal Bureau of Investigation, viz. Diagnosis probable. Admitted time such and such, place such and such, patient's residence such and such.' And after me watching those crazy tickers

for ten years, the bright Mr. Herron from the FBI tells
me that this ain't no code!"

"Have you tried reading it backward?" said the cop
with the holster.

"I have," said Starkey. "By God, I have."

At that moment the buzzing and ticking from the next
room stopped dead. Communications was quiet as a library. The three men in the little room held their breaths.
Herron slopped some coffee. Suddenly the clatter exploded again. They looked at each other and the cop with
the holster made a noise in his throat.

"As I was saying…" he said.

That's when the door from Communications flew open
and Jones looked in.

"Your message, Starkey. It's on the ticker."

Herron and Starkey ran to the teletype. It was still
hammering with a nervous beat and the message read:
"Diagnosis probable. Admitted 10:15 p.m., Hamilton
City Hospital, Hamilton City. Patient's residence, 24
Chester Street, Hamilton City." When Starkey tore
off the sheet, Herron was already halfway out of the
door. He'd got his message. A hundred miles away they'd
found the first victim. Finally the trail was hot. Real hot.
The patient had radiation sickness.

Cal and Tom hadn't known each other for more than a
few hours but they had been stepping fast. They'd been
stepping so fast that by midnight it seemed they'd been
buddies all their lives. That's why Cal had been buying
the drinks for Tom and then Tom had been buying the
drinks for Cal. So it was a sad moment when the two
buddies sat down at the curb and discovered that their
friendship was wearing thin.

"Stop rubbing them stubbles," said Cal. "You trying to drive me crazy with them stubble noises?"

Tom kept rubbing his stubbles and said, "Bah."

They sat for a while staring at the dark street and then they looked at the empty pint in the gutter. That brought up the next point.

"Cheapskate," said Cal. "Just lookit this empty pint."

"Cheapskate!" Tom jumped up from the curb. He stood straight and steady after a while and yelled, "Cheapskate! You're talking to the man what bought that pint, ya bum!"

"It's empty, ain't it?"

"So it's your turn, ya bum! It's your turn for the next one."

Cal got up from the curb and held himself by Tom's sleeve. "Listen, cheapskate," he said. He stuck his face close to Tom's. Tom tried to lean back and out of the way. "I got the pint afore this one and I barely recall buying that pint and it's empty. Then I barely recall this pint coming along and it's empty. Unnerstand?"

Tom didn't. He tried to lean his face out of the way and they both started to sway.

"So it's your turn," Cal said, and it sounded like a conclusion.

They swayed for a while, staring at each other from close range, but Tom didn't know what to say next.

"I knew it," said Cal. "You're a cheapskate. You stink!"

Tom jerked his head back and wiped his eye. "Don't say 'stink' like that. A bum what can't talk polite never gets nowheres."

He took a few steps and leaned against a dark store window. It made a dangerous sound. Then Cal came over and leaned against the glass. They looked inside as best they could.

"More cheapskates," said Cal. "The whole store full of bulbs and wires and no light anywhere."

"That's because he sells 'em," Tom said.

They looked at the display of fixtures, bulbs, and fluorescent tubes. There was a display of fluorescent tubes like sun rays coming out from a face in the middle. The cardboard face was smiling.

"What's he got to smile about I can't figure," said Cal.

"He's thinking of that drink he's gonna have. He believes in miracles and he's just smiling away there, thinking—"

Tom didn't get any further because Cal had burst out crying, loud and hard, sobbing that he'd always believed in miracles, but not anymore.

"Cal boy! Cal buddy! You're busting my heart, honest, Cal boy." Then he patted his buddy on the back and gradually his face got stern. "Cal!"

"Yes, Tommy?"

"We got to have a miracle."

"There ain't—"

"First guy comes along we ask for a miracle, Cal buddy."

Cal had stopped crying. He felt like himself again. "Maybe an angel's gonna come down the street? Carrying a pint?"

"Shut up. Here he comes!" and they both listened to the footsteps that came down the dark street. They were coming at a fast clip.

"Or maybe Jesus Christ Himself."

"Shut up already and get over here!" Tom dragged his buddy to the entrance to the house next to the electrical store. "Here comes the miracle. Watch me make a touch."

"Oh, surely. Maybe Jesus Christ—" He stopped when they saw the figure come through the dark.

Tom stepped into the street, all energy and smiles. "How do you do, sir? I do believe—" He got no further. The man was at the window now when a sudden glow of eerie white suffused the dark. The display of fluorescent bulbs glowed brilliantly, and against the sudden brightness the dark figure of the man appeared surrounded by a halo.

"Jesus Christ!" Cal said, and fell down on his face.

Tom hadn't moved a muscle. By the time he managed to breathe again, the lights were off and the middle-aged man in the blue overcoat had gripped his yellow leather case and run into the night.

Tony Catell hurried up the stairs of the railroad station and pushed his way through the crowd without looking right or left. Once inside, he went to the far end of the large hall, where the ornamental columns made shadowed recesses along the wall. He stood there watching the ticket windows. When one of them was empty, Catell walked over and bought a ticket to Detroit.

Twenty minutes to traintime.

Catell went to the short-order counter and sat down, but the seat faced the wrong way. He got up again, walked to the other side of the U-shaped counter, and found a seat that faced the entrance of the station. With a slight turn he could also see the gateways that led to the trains. He put his yellow leather case on the floor under the counter and ordered a glass of milk. After he had finished the milk he smoked a cigarette, ordered another glass of milk, and watched the waitress behind the counter. She was young, but nothing special. Catell watched her for the same reason he drank a lot of milk. He hadn't had much of either for the past eight years.

Without moving his head, Catell glanced at the waitress, the entrance, the crowds, and then at the waitress again, but there was no particular expression on his face. He looked tired and lined. His long jaw had a bluish cast that made the rest of his face look like the color of wet chalk. A small muscle jumped in his cheek, but otherwise Catell sat quite still.

Ten minutes to traintime.

Catell picked specks of dust from the sleeve of his blue overcoat and wondered whether to order another glass of milk. But suddenly the thought made him sick. His forehead glistened with sudden sweat and he swallowed hard. Then the nausea passed.

Perhaps he was overdoing the milk. Catell rubbed his pale forehead. His whole face was pale, very pale. Catell hadn't been out of prison very long.

Five minutes before traintime he paid the waitress and got up. Carrying his yellow leather case, he started for one of the train gates.

A redcap walked up behind him. "Carry that for you?" The redcap put his hand on the case.

Catell jumped. "Let go."

But the redcap didn't catch the tone of Catell's voice, and he reached for the leather case again. That's when Catell spun on the balls of his feet, his fist thudding into the porter's stomach. Before anybody had seen a thing, Catell was walking toward the train gate, his thin face a mask, his movements controlled. The redcap lay on the floor, doubled over in groaning pain. For all of his fifty years, Tony Catell was very fast and very strong.

One minute before traintime he entered his compartment and locked the door. When the train started to move, he put the leather case on the seat, took off his hat and coat, and sat down. It was hours before the train would hit Detroit, but Catell did not make himself comfortable. He sat without leaning against the cushions, his narrow hands folded between his knees, only his eyes showing how tired he was. He hadn't slept much during the past few days, because he had been nervous and unsure of himself. When Schumacher had explained the heist to him, Catell had felt unsure. The feeling had stayed with him when he had cased the job, when he had pulled it, and when he had haled up in that burg Hamilton City for a few hours of fitful sleep.

The job had been too easy. Catell pulled out a cigarette and then forgot to light it. He wondered if prison could have made him feel this way, broken down to the size of a gutless punk, a nervous rat. But that didn't make sense, because he had been in prison before. He was a three-time loser, out for the last time, out for good until he died— one way or the other.

Catell jumped in his seat and made an automatic move for the leather case next to him. He had fallen asleep there, sitting there with the doubt and the fear scrambling his brain.

He cursed through his teeth, trying to shake the weariness out of his bones. He was getting too old, maybe, a crazy has-been who was trying to wrench himself back up by dreams of an old reputation; a reputation so old it didn't even fit the picture any more. He had slipped badly; he'd slipped so hard that they'd sent him up for that third time.

But that was going to be the end of that. They didn't know it yet but they had given him his other chance. Nobody was going to call Catell a has-been, an old broken-down three-time loser with a lot of fancy memories and a long list of dead friends.

He was going to pull that big one once more, the one that only Tony Catell could handle, the job that meant big time. And he wanted to walk away from it with a bundle. Perhaps this heist had looked so easy because he still had that old touch. And he certainly had walked away with a solid piece of swag. He patted the briefcase beside him. There was nothing small time about its contents, a thirty-six-pound ingot of solid gold.

Chapter Two

Otto Schumacher chewed his gray mustache and pushed his glass back and forth on the table. He looked across the crowded room of the roadhouse, but he didn't focus on anything in particular.

"What time is it, Selma?"

"Eleven. Five minutes later than the last time you asked me."

Schumacher hardly heard the woman. He was nervous; he disliked public places.

"Otto, lemme have another drink." Selma waited a moment for an answer and then waved for a waiter.

She got her drink and rolled a little bit of the liquid on her tongue. She liked the fine sharp sting in her mouth.

"Otto, how about another one for you?"

Schumacher looked at his glass, half full with a tepid brown liquid.

"No, thanks. You have one."

"I just got one."

"Good. Good. Anything you want, Selma."

"I want a hot-water bottle."

"Fine. Fine, Selma."

"I want two hot-water bottles, you bum!"

"You want— Selma, what are you talking about?"

Selma looked at Schumacher as if he were a sick dog and made an ugly sound in her throat. Then she swallowed her drink.

"Selma, what was that for?"

"For you, lovin' cup. I want another drink."

"You're the one that wanted to come. I told you this was strictly business, but you had to tag along."

"That's right, lovin' cup. I had to tag along to this converted hash joint. I had to tag along. That's how much fun I get hanging around you, lovin' cup."

"Selma, I have spoken to you before and I will speak again. I give you anything, the best—"

"With you, the best ain't much, lovin' cup."

"You're no spring chicken yourself, dear Selma." There was a short silence. They didn't look at each other.

"I want another drink."

Schumacher went to the bar to buy Selma another drink. He was disgusted with himself for losing his temper. Besides, Selma was all right, a fine woman to have around. Just right, now that she was slowing down a little.

He brought the drink back to the booth and noticed that Selma was getting tight. The little wrinkles around her eyes showed up more clearly and one of her curls was hanging down the side of her ear.

"Selma, I got business tonight and I must ask you to go easy. You know what it means to us."

"Yeah. I bet he won't show."

Schumacher narrowed his eyes for a moment. "He'll show. I've known Tony for twenty years and he'll show."

"And what if he shows and the deal didn't come off?"

"The deal came off all right, Selma."

"So what are you worried about? Why do you have to sit there like a fireplug the dog passed by?"

"It's not that simple. There's some trouble."

"Oh, sure. Schumacher, the brains from way back, he gets himself the best jug heavy in the field, his old buddy Tony Catell, who, just fresh from college, is eager to please his old buddy Otto, and he sets him up with a setup like happens once in a lifetime, he sets him up. And when Tony delivers the goods, all of a sudden there is some trouble. With you, Schumacher, there is always some trouble!"

Schumacher didn't answer. If she didn't stop shouting and making scenes, he'd tell her to beat it for good. He'd tell her she was through and she could pick her stuff up in the morning. Off the sidewalk, where he'd throw it. Schumacher turned toward Selma but she wasn't saying a thing now. Her lidded eyes were wide open, her thin mouth was smiling vaguely, and her chin was tilted up as if she were looking over somebody's head. Selma was patting her tight curls and then Schumacher saw Tony Catell in the crowd.

He was slowly worming his way past the bar, around the crowded tables, and up to the booth. Catell walked past the booth without a sign of recognition. He went to the men's room, came back to the booth, and sat down.

"What's she here for?"

"Otto and I are always together," Selma said, and she put her hand through Schumacher's arm. She leaned forward on the table and smiled at Catell. He looked at the V of her dress. Selma was small there. What Catell remembered about Selma was her fine skin and her wide hips. He saw she still had a fine smooth skin.

"My boy, I congratulate you," Schumacher said. "That was a fine job you did there."

"Thanks. You figured a neat setup. No troubles."

"That's what I wanted to speak to you about, Tony. We're not quite through yet. The fact is—"

Tony wasn't listening. His white face looked worn with sleeplessness and his hands were nervous.

"Lemme have a drink first, Otto. I'm beat."

"That's right, lovin' cup. Let him have a drink first, for chrissakes. You and your business all hours of the day and night. I'll have one with you, Tony." Selma smiled at him again.

Schumacher didn't say anything. Above all, he wanted to keep peace. It was difficult enough to explain things to Tony without Selma acting up.

When the drinks had come, Schumacher cleared his throat and said, "Tony, pay attention. Something slipped up."

Catell only shifted his eyes. "Nothing slipped. Nobody saw me, nobody followed me, nobody knows I'm here in Detroit. And we got the gold, didn't we? Selma, want another drink?"

She smiled at him and pushed her glass toward him. Before she leaned back in her seat she touched his sleeve and ran one finger along the back of his hand.

"How about you, Otto? Another drink?" Catell said.

Schumacher shook his head and swirled the brown liquid in his glass. He didn't like the way things were going.

"Listen, Tony," he said. "This trouble we got is the kind you wouldn't know anything about."

"What trouble? We got the gold and nobody knows it. What more do you want?"

Schumacher leaned forward in his seat and stared at Catell with an exasperated look on his face. "What do I want? I want to sell the stuff, that's what I want. And the trouble is, I can't sell it now!"

"What?"

"I said we can't sell it. That gold is radioactive."

"What in hell are you talking about?"

"I'm trying to explain. When I staked out the job, I didn't get the full story. I didn't know that gold would be radioactive. I just found out."

Catell understood two things: He understood that Schumacher said he couldn't sell the gold, and he understood that Schumacher was serious. He could tell by the old man's face, by his sick-looking eyes, and by the way Schumacher sat hunched forward in his overcoat. Why didn't the old bastard ever take his overcoat off? What was he trying to pull with his double talk? Catell's brain was too tired to think straight. All he could do was sit there and hate Schumacher, hate his reasonable ways, his messy-looking mustache, his slut Selma, who kept grinning at him with her big face.

"Catell, are you listening to me?"

"Yeah." He took his eyes off Selma's naked arm and forced himself to concentrate. "All right, Schumacher, what's this crap about radioactive? The stuff is gold, isn't it?"

"Jesus, Catell, don't you know what radioactive is? That metal is pure poison!"

Catell held the whisky glass up to his mouth and licked the rim with a slow motion of his tongue. When he looked at Schumacher, his eyes glittered with fatigue. "Otto, are you giving me the runaround?"

Schumacher caught the tone of Catell's voice and he had a bad moment. Then he talked with a voice that was harsh and hurried.

"I don't think you understand, Catell. That ingot of metal you got is dangerous. It gives off radiations that can make a man sick, and for all I know, it can kill a man. Now shut up for a minute. When this deal came up, all I knew was that the government was shipping one ingot of gold to the Atomic Research Center of Kelvin University. The gold was going to be there about a week and they were going to do some kind of fancy radiation work on the thing. When, how, why, and so forth—that I didn't know, except that I had a good idea it wasn't going to be during the first two days. That's why I planned the heist for the second day after the gold got there. Well, the setup was good and you came through as expected. The setup was real good. They got their security rules and so on, but the work at that research place isn't really so secret. They only do limited work and nothing very new. So it doesn't call for full-dress security. Besides, it's a university and no Fort Knox. So the whole deal worked out easy as pie except now we are stuck with a worthless chunk of gold."

Catell took a deep breath, with an effort. When he spoke his voice sounded squeezed. "Otto, how come you know so much? How come it's on again, off again, and nobody knows but you?"

Schumacher started to toss his hands in exasperation. Then he stopped as if the gesture had exhausted him.

"Tony, for God's sake, I'm telling you straight. Something slipped and the bar you got was already hot. You're worried how come I know so much? From the horse's mouth I know, straight from the FBI bulletins on the radio, ads in the papers, and all of them screaming that the loot you got is radioactive. They send out warnings. Haven't you read it or heard it?"

"I haven't had time to read the papers."

"All right, so I'm telling you. When radioactive stuff disappears, maybe stolen, they right away put out a total alarm. To you, to the guy that's toting that dangerous stuff around and doesn't know it." Schumacher leaned back in his seat and unbuttoned his overcoat. He was sweating.

"So listen to me, Tony, and listen to reason. We don't know how hot that gold is, perhaps just a little, but it's poison just the same. We've got to stay clear of it and we can't move it right now. Not for a while. That radioactivity wears off in time, so it'll safe again after a while, but right now—" Schumacher made a helpless gesture.

Suddenly Catell felt so weary he could have lain down in the booth and slept. He felt that if he couldn't sleep right now he might cry.

"The deal's got to be canceled," Schumacher was saying. "It came off good but it ended up bad. Later, maybe. Right now it's a flop."

The words came to Catell like a curse. They stung him with a fine, deep pain that gripped his body and shook him awake. He gritted his teeth and leaned toward Schumacher.

"And now I'll say my piece. I don't know about this radioactive crap, Otto, and it's not going to scare me. It may be true what you say, and then again it may not. I've been toting this stuff around and nothing's happened to to me. If it's rotten or if it's hot, that stuff won't stop me, because I'm not stopping. Get that, Otto. Nothing's going to stop me and I wouldn't want you to be the one to try it."

He took a deep breath. He felt all right again.

"Selma," he said, "how's it been for excitement?"

He was glad Selma was there. Right then he felt she was the sexiest female he had ever seen. He didn't notice the wrinkles around her heavy eyes or the loose skin under her chin. He just saw her big face, which had been very handsome, and he noticed her white arms, which still had beautiful skin.

"How about a dance, kid?" he said.

"Tony," Schumacher said, "where's the gold?"

"Oh, leave him alone now, Otto. Can't you ever stop talking business?"

"She's right, Otto. We'll talk tomorrow. We don't need to push that stuff in this town. So we get rid of it some-place else. We'll figure some other way. We won't let this thing die on the vine, eh, Otto?"

This was the first time Catell had smiled in a long time. But he wasn't looking at Otto. Selma smiled back at him and started to push her way out of the booth.

"Tony," said Schumacher, "where's that rotten gold?"

"Lemme out, Otto. Tony wants to dance with me." Selma pushed against Schumacher's side.

"Let the lady out, Otto," Tony said. He got up, taking Schumacher by the arm.

"All right, Tony, all right. Go dance. But where'd you stash that gold? You got to tell me."

Tony had pulled Schumacher to his feet and Selma got out of the booth. She stood close to Catell and didn't move when he put his arm around her and dug his fingers into the flesh of her waist.

"The loot is safe, Otto. I left it at your place."

"At my place? How'd you get in?"

"How'd I get in!" He laughed at Schumacher's worried face.

"Tony, get it out of there, man. I'm telling you it's dangerous stuff." He clutched at Catell's arm.

"Let go," Catell said, and he gave Schumacher a vicious push.

The older man sat down in his seat with a thump and looked up at the couple. "Selma, you reason with him," he said. "You and I aren't safe with that thing around. He's got to get it out."

"What makes you think I won't be safe?" Selma said, and her smile was hazy with alcohol.

Catell made an impatient gesture. "I'll move it. Don't worry. Otto. I'll move it in a day or so, once I get my bearings." He gave Selma a sharp squeeze and pushed her ahead of him toward the dance floor.

"Tony!" Schumacher called after the couple. "Tony, tonight. Please do it tonight!" But nobody heard him. He sat hunched in the booth and followed the couple with his eyes. They did not dance. They skirted the dance floor and went out the front door.

After a while, Schumacher thought of ordering a fresh drink for himself, but decided against it. He hated drinking in public places, and he hated this place in particular. He sat and waited only because he was afraid to go home. He waited, hoping Catell would come back and agree to move that ingot out of the apartment tonight.

When the band packed up, Schumacher got up and left. There was no point in waiting any longer. Catell must have taken Selma to town.

Outside, Schumacher shivered in his overcoat and smoothed a finger over his gray mustache. He felt cold and alone. With an old man's awkwardness he hunted in his pockets for the car key. When he had found it, he walked into the parking lot.

Before he put his hand on the door, Schumacher felt the car move. In the back seat he saw them. He saw Catell's back and he saw one of Selma's legs.

Schumacher left quietly, thinking with dread of the dreary bus ride home, and of the thing that waited for him there.

Chapter Three

Jack Herron didn't much like to go on a case with his chief. It made him uncomfortable and awkward. Jones never said much and always wore a bland face. Without talking they walked down the main corridor of the Research Center of Kelvin University until they came to a door marked "C. A. Tiffin, Director." At the Research Center, Tiffin was top dog. He was bald, thin, and ugly, but he was top dog and he always let you know it.

"Well, gentlemen, what have you done about this outrage besides handicapping our work at the Center? I suppose you have come back for another one of your double checks?"

"Outrage, Dr. Tiffin?"

"The theft, Mr. Jones. The almost unbelievable—"

"We're handling that matter. For the moment we are concerned with another aspect of the—uh—outrage; the aspect that was your responsibility."

"I beg your pardon?"

"The drained shielding wall around your atomic pile. The radiation leak that made the stored gold radioactive in the first place. Have you determined just how radioactive the ingot may have been at the time of the theft?"

Tiffin shuffled his papers around. He pushed his chair back abruptly and stood.

"The difficulties are such—" he started.

"Have you figured it out?"

"My assistants are still working on it, Mr. Jones."

Jones shrugged. "Before we leave, please show us the scene of the theft once again, Dr. Tiffin." He held the door open.

They walked through the central hall of the building and turned into a corridor. It was long and bare.

"There is not much to see," said Tiffin. "Our atomic pile is small, extending from about here to here." He paced off close to forty feet in the corridor and pointed to one blank wall. "The room housing the device is completely shielded. Follow me, please."

They turned the corner of the corridor and Tiffin opened a door. A wooden sign stood next to it, face to the wall. Herron turned it around and read, "Danger. Radioactivity."

"It's quite safe now. The sign was only put there after the leak was discovered. Ordinarily this room is not exposed. Follow me, please."

The small room held racks and a trapdoor in one wall. There was moisture on the floor.

"This wall," Tiffin said, "shields the business end of the pile from the storage room in which we stand. The wall is actually a series of large canisters filled with water. Sometime during the day previous to the theft, this drainpipe—you can see it near the floor—seems to have leaked water out of the lower series of tanks."

"And there was nothing in this room except the gold ingot?"

"Nothing else. That's why we cannot say for how much time, if any, the gold was subject to bombardment."

"So it may not be radioactive at all."

"Possibly. Or it may be only partially radioactive."

"How do you mean, partially?" Herron wanted to know.

"Only a part of its mass, let's say a fraction of an inch on the surface, may have become radioactive. Which would be a blessing," Tiffin added. "That is, if you can find it at all."

"We'll find what's left of it," Jones said.

"Left of it? What are you talking about, Chief?" Herron asked.

"Irradiated gold," Tiffin said, and he sounded indulgent, "has a half-life of one day. That means that after a day has passed, its radioactivity has reduced itself by half; the following day there is again a reduction to half of what was left, and so on. What remains, young man, is not gold. What remains is pure stable mercury."

"You mean nothing may be left to that stuff except quicksilver?"

"Hardly, Mr. Herron. That kind of total deterioration of a large ingot would require more energy than our pile can muster. And besides, the thief wouldn't have left here alive."

"That's good to know," said Herron. "So we're still looking for gold."

"Considering our source of radiation and the possible length of time the ingot may have been exposed, the affected part of the gold would be quite small, but nonetheless dangerous. Of course, once the radiation has dissipated itself, the body of the ingot is again quite harmless. Pure gold, with traces of mercury."

They left the storage room and went back to Tiffin's office.

"Will there be anything else?" Tiffin stopped by the door.

"Just your report, Dr. Tiffin. We must know how sick the thief may be, and how dangerous the ingot may be to the population."

"Mr. Jones, our guess as to how long the gold was exposed may not help you as much as you think. Nonlethal doses of radiation may cause a variety of symptoms, and they may appear to be harmless things."

"What are they?" Jones asked.

"In general, the first signs are weariness, headache, digestive upset. The mucosa of the digestive tract seems particularly sensitive to radiation. Sometimes skin irritations occur, like a sunburn. In severe cases skin ulcerations develop or simple sores that refuse to heal. The most specific effect, of course, is the destruction of bone marrow with consequent blood deterioration. After that, any infection becomes a serious matter. But I'm sure you knew all this."

"That much we knew, Dr. Tiffin. In the meantime, please hurry with your report."

"I don't see how a mere guess—"

"An intelligent guess, Dr. Tiffin. Good day, sir."

Herron thought Jones had done that very well. He followed his chief down the long corridor and out into the open. The sun was shining and some new flowerbeds made a good smell in the air. Herron was glad to be out of the building. There hadn't been any windows in the place.

They walked across the campus to the parking lot while Herron kept thinking about the things Tiffin had said.

"Has anybody answered our alarm yet, Chief?"

"Hundreds of hypochondriacs."

"At least we'll have our man worried."

"Not necessarily, Herron. If he's got half a brain, he'll keep from exposing himself after hearing our alarm, and any mild symptoms he might get he'd be apt to overlook at first."

"Till it gets worse."

"It might, Herron. A few repeated exposures, each one

of them small, and the effect will grow. At any rate, what have you found out in the meantime?"

Herron pulled a notebook out of his breast pocket and began to recite.

"Besides the Hamilton City case of radiation, no further reports, and they're not sure it is radiation burn. Three of our sources report heavy spending by two of the suspects, Ham Lippin and Jerald Jenner. Ham is in Miami Beach and Jerry is in San Diego. I also got that list of parolees you asked for. It narrows down to seven: the two Corvetti brothers, Sam Nutchin, Gus Eisenberg, Tony Catell, Carl Lamotte, and Mug McFarlane. Three of them aren't very likely, considering everything. Sam Nutchin is very sick, Tony Catell is a has-been without connections, and one of the Corvettis is drunk most of the time. So that leaves us with the younger Corvetti, Eisenberg, Lamotte, and McFarlane."

"That leaves us with a lot of nothing."

"Sorry, Chief, that's as far as I could get, so far."

They walked in silence till they came to the parking lot behind the library.

"Have the two watchmen come up with anything else?" Jones asked.

"Same story. Somebody slugged them from behind. They don't know whether there was one or more assailants."

"How are they getting along?"

"No change. Bad concussions."

"Any new evidence that the lab boys dug up?"

"They find evidence of one person only."

Jones and Herron got into the car. Jones took the wheel.

"Seems like quite an order for one man," Herron said.

"Two watchmen slugged, three doors jimmied, two electric-eye circuits ruined, one vault door blown, not to speak of the missing gold."

"What might help us is the fact that the loot could be radioactive. I hate to think of it, Jack, but that might make it more convenient for us to track it down."

"It hasn't so far, Chief."

"I know. But a thirty-six-pound block of radioactive gold is going to make somebody sick."

"Yeah. Especially since the thief probably didn't know the stuff could be radioactive. If he'd known, he wouldn't have kept the stuff in the same room with him when he holed up in that crummy rooming house in Hamilton City."

"That may not mean a thing. Don't forget, we still haven't a trace of the thief or the gold, which probably means he hasn't slowed down any himself."

The drive from Kelvin University back to St. Louis took them one hour, but at the end of that time, neither Jones nor Herron had come up with any new ideas. When the trip was over and they pulled into the underground garage of headquarters, they were glad to get out of the car. Herron looked rumpled and tired, but Jones appeared as bland and neat as ever.

"Who knows, perhaps we'll have a break when we get to the office, eh, Chief?"

Jones smiled back for a moment, but didn't answer. They took the elevator to their floor and entered the bureau.

"Come to my office, will you, Jack? I want you to look at the follow-ups I got on some of the possible brains behind this job. Right now we're going on the assumption that this was not a syndicate job."

"Why?"

"Lots of reasons. For instance, they would have used more than one man at the scene. I'll show you the analysis later. Now, as I was saying, that narrows the field quite a bit. There aren't too many independents left."

Herron opened the door for Jones and they walked into the Chief's office.

"All right, Jack. Here's a dossier on Charles Letterman, alias Chauncey Lettre, alias Professor Letters. Sixty-five years old, convicted twice for complicity in bank robberies. Light sentence each time. One conviction for illegal possession of stolen goods. He's suspected of planning a long list of crimes. Take a look at it. Present address, Two-o-seven Desbrosses Street, New York City. Next, there's one Otto Schumacher, sixty-eight, no aliases. A very careful planner. When you look at the list, you'll find he's supposedly been behind a lot of inside jobs, but don't let that prejudice you. Otherwise, little is known about him except that he was probably behind some of the biggest heists during the twenties. And he's never been convicted of anything. Take the file along, Jack, and hold it, because we haven't found him yet."

The phone rang. Jones picked it up and said, "Jones." He listened for a while, then said, "Good. Thanks." He put the receiver down and told Herron not to bother with the other dossiers. "Just read the one on Otto Schumacher. They found him. It seems he spent last month in Kelvin, presumably to use the university library. He roomed at the same house as one of the night watchmen of the Research Center, and they often played checkers together. At present he lives in Detroit, where the local office has him staked out. They're going to pull him in tomorrow, and I want you to be there. We have little to go on with

Schumacher except that his cleaning woman showed up at the county clinic today. Complaint, headache and diarrhea, plus a possible radiation burn of the sole of one foot. Could be a coincidence, though. He's your case, Jack, but remember, he's never been convicted. Good luck."

"Good luck, Otto. I think I found a contact out West who'll take the stuff."

"Tony, for God's sake, where have you been." Schumacher yelled into the phone. His hands were shaking. "Do you realize that damn thing is still in this apartment? Have you any idea what a time I had trying to keep from going nuts waiting for you? Either you come at once or I'll get somebody else to take it out of here. Tony, are you listening?!"

There was a short silence at the other end of the wire and then Catell's voice, very quiet: "Don't do it, Otto. I'm warning you."

"All right, all right. Are you coming?"

"I'll be there, Otto. Have you moved it any?"

"Are you insane? I haven't—"

"Don't blubber, Otto You could have done something to shield it. I heard lead—"

"For God's sake, Tony, get over here and don't lecture me. I haven't been able to think straight with that thing under the floor!"

"I'll be over, Otto. I got a lead apron from a guy, like they wear when they take X rays. We'll wrap it in that. I'll be there this afternoon."

Schumacher sighed with relief and wiped his forehead. "Thank God. Make it soon, Tony. I'll be waiting. Ah, Tony …are you in town, Tony?"

"Yeah. Why?"

"Nothing Just make it soon. And Tony—"

"Yeah, what is it?"

"Ah, everything O.K. with you?"

"Sure, sure. See you later, Otto."

"Tony, is Selma all right? Tony?"

But the line was dead. Schumacher put down the receiver and walked to the window. Four stories down he saw three kids playing with a ball. Two of them were tossing the ball back and forth and the third kid was trying to catch it away from them. Then a man walked up and caught the ball out of the air. He put it in his pocket and turned down the street, the three kids running after him.

Schumacher left the window and wiped his forehead again. He went to the kitchen to get a drink of water, then changed his mind. Schumacher felt sickish and sticky.

There were three rooms in the apartment and Schumacher kept pacing back and forth from the living room to the bedroom, from the bedroom to the living room. The third room was closed and Schumacher didn't go near it. Nobody had been in the room since Catell had come back, except for the cleaning woman. Schumacher had found her standing near the bookshelf, dusting and humming a tune. He argued with her from the doorway to come out and leave his books alone. He screamed at her and she screamed back, but she didn't move from her spot till she finished dusting the books. Right under her feet, under the flooring, lay the radioactive gold.

Schumacher remembered the incident and looked at the closed door. The thought of that silent yellow thing, radiating death with no noise, no odor, no natural signs at all, made him feel clammy. "I'm cracking," he mumbled. "I've got to hold on, for God's sake."

He went to the bathroom and turned on the cold water. When he leaned over to wash his face, his vision blurred and he lost his balance. Schumacher grabbed the washbowl with both hands, but his head slammed into the cabinet over the basin. The sudden pain cleared his head and he felt better. Straightening he inhaled deeply, but his eyes refused to focus. He doubled over, a sharp cramp twisting his insides, and retched. He retched till he thought his head would split with the pressure. When it was over, Schumacher staggered from the bathroom, found the front window, and pulled it open. He leaned over the windowsill and took greedy breaths of the fresh, cool air. After a while his strength came back, and with it the horror of the knowledge that he was sick. Not just sick like anyone else, but sick with the hard live rays from the radioactive gold. His mouth shook.

When his head cleared, Schumacher looked up and down the street. He saw nobody. What happened to the kids with the ball? What happened to those people who usually stood on house steps, walked down streets, loitered at corners? But there were people loitering at the corner. There were two men at each corner.

Seized with a sudden hunger, Schumacher went to the kitchen and ate a plate of cold stew, some dry bread, and a few spoons of peanut butter. Then he went back to the living room and lit himself a cigar. The window was still open. Now there were three men at one corner and none at the other. A closed truck had pulled up to the curb near the fireplug next to the corner. And there were two men walking toward the house where Schumacher had his apartment. One was smoking a cigarette, the other was carrying a small, square satchel.

*

"What time is it?" The one with the cigarette sounded nervous.

"Five to three."

"They should be at the back now, you think?"

"Give them another few minutes."

They started down the street slowly. The one with the satchel opened the top of the leather case and flicked the switch for a dial that showed through the opening. Immediately the box began a faint and intermittent crackling.

"Turn that damn thing down, man. You wanna arouse the whole block?"

"Take it easy. You can hardly hear it. What's the matter with your nerves, anyway?"

"Nothing. There's nothing wrong with my nerves."

"You scared of this Schumacher, maybe? He's over sixty, you know. Here, have another cigarette."

"Thanks "

"Well? Go ahead and smoke it."

"For chrissakes, stop picking on me. In case you and that damn box there haven't heard, Schumacher's got a reputation that goes back to when you were tripping over your diapers. And turn that crazy ticker off, or whatever it is."

"Can't do that, Harry It's science. And science never—"

"Aw, shut up!"

They walked without talking for a while. Only the traffic at the ends of the street made a noise, and the box they had along. Every so often it ticked and crackled.

"Why's that damn thing ticking all the time? Is everything radioactive, for chrissakes?"

"This is nothing. You should hear it tick when there's hot stuff around. But I guess you won't hear it perform today. Schumacher would be crazy to keep that gold around. What time now?"

"Three sharp."

"O.K., let's go."

"Wait!"

At the end of the street where the closed truck was parked a man had appeared and seemed about to enter the short street. The driver of the truck climbed out of his cab and started toward the man. The stranger stopped, bent toward the wall of a building, and lit a cigarette. Then he continued past the street and disappeared.

"Thank God," said the man with the Geiger counter. "For a minute I thought that guy in the blue coat was coming this way. All right, let's go. We stay in the hall for ten minutes while the guys from the back go upstairs and check the corridors. Then Herron joins us and we go up."

"I just hope that guy in the blue coat doesn't decide to come back."

Tony Catell had spent his life trying to avoid trouble, and he had developed a sharp nose for it. When he turned into Schumacher's street something brought him up short. There weren't enough people. It was too quiet. Two guys down the block were walking too slowly.

Cops.

Catell controlled a panicky urge to run and took a step toward the wall of the nearest building. He lit a cigarette. Looking over his cupped hands, he saw a man climb out of a truck, turn toward him, and stop. The guy wasn't sure, but he was watching. Who did they want? Schumacher? Himself? Suddenly a strong hot hate boiled up inside him, killing his doubt, his fear, his short moment of hesitation.

Nothing was going to get in his way, nothing! Catell didn't
wonder how they had found Schumacher, whether they
knew the gold was there, or whether they knew about him.
He didn't even stop to figure what to do, or how, or when.
Catell turned into a thing possessed with one thought
only: Get that gold!

He had lit a cigarette to make his stop at the corner
seem natural. He walked on so they wouldn't bother to
look at him. And then he saw the delivery car. It was
parked in the driveway a few yards ahead, and on the
side of the car was lettered "TV Repair." The driver was
opening the door in the rear.

It took Catell a few quick steps to get behind the man
at the truck and less than a second to jab his hand, stiff
fingered, into the driver's right kidney. The man didn't
scream. He exhaled with a rattle in his throat and started
to sag. Catell jerked the rear door open, tossed the man
in, and jumped after him. Without bothering to close the
door, he smashed his fist into the groaning face and the
man went limp. Catell took off his hat and coat, ripped
the jacket and cap off the unconscious driver, and put
them on. Then he jumped out the back. Whistling a tune,
he slammed the back door shut, jumped in the driver's
seat, and drove back to the corner that he had just left.

Catell pulled around the corner fast, skimming the
parked truck by inches. The unconscious man in the back
rolled heavily against a television set. Glass broke and
picture tubes without their housings crashed around the
floor. Catell came to a sharp stop in front of Schumacher's
house and, still whistling, jumped out of the truck and
opened the door in the back. With one hand he pulled
the television set toward him; with the other he reached
for a wrench. A few sharp blows and the tube in the set

was broken, leaving a large, empty space. Carrying the set in both arms, Catell slammed the rear door with his foot and went up the stairs of the apartment house. Catell kept on whistling loudly, even when he saw faces looking at him through the glass of the door.

Cops.

Again he didn't have to think, to decide.

"Is one of you jerks going to open that door?"

For a moment they didn't move, just stared at the man with the television set. Through the glass Catell saw the lips of one of them move, and he seemed to be saying, "Of all the rotten luck—"

The one with the cigarette opened the door and Catell went through. He gave the man with the cigarette a push with the back of the television set.

"Pardon me, buster. Step aside." He went to the stairs and up, whistling as before.

He didn't see an agent on every floor, but he knew they were there. They didn't worry him. The one on the fourth floor—he'd have to get rid of him.

When Catell came to Schumacher's door, he looked down the corridor and saw a man busying himself with the hallway window. The guy was concentrating very hard on the window.

"Hey, buddy," Catell said.

"You calling me?"

"Yeah. Gimme a hand, willya?"

That's the guy he had to get rid of. When the agent came closer, Catell pushed the television set at him.

"Hold this for a second, buddy?"

The man put his arms around the bulky cabinet and looked at Catell with a question, but just as he was going to say something, Catell's arm whipped out and the ridge of his hand slashed across the man's Adam's apple. That was all there was to it. Catell caught the set and let the man drop. Then he kicked his foot against Schumacher's door.

"Open up. It's Tony."

Schumacher pulled the door open a crack.

"Open up quick. Drag that cop in here." Catell pushed past Schumacher into the apartment. "Don't stand there, goddamn it, get that guy on the floor there!"

Schumacher dragged the unconscious man from the hall and kicked the door shut.

"Tony, what goes here? Did you say 'cop'?"

"Quick, where's the stuff? Same place?"

"Of course. You didn't think I was going to go near—"

"Shut up and listen. The place is lousy with cops. Feds, I think. The whole street is staked out. Now I'm going to take this stuff and walk right out of here. You stay put. They got nothing on you, they don't find nothing, and you don't say nothing. Understand? I'll contact you."

Catell went to his knees before the bookcase and pulled up the rug. Then he lifted three boards, stuck his hand inside the hole, and dragged out the battered yellow cartridge case he had hidden there. When he lifted it, something thumped inside the locked case.

"Wanna take a quick look, Otto?" Catell started to undo the latch.

"For God's sake, Tony, leave it closed. That gold is poison, Tony. It's poison of the worst kind."

Catell had shoved the box inside the television set and started toward the door.

"Tony, I beg you, I beg you to listen—"

"Out of my way!"

Catell had his hands full with the cabinet. He kicked

at Schumacher with his foot and caught him on the shin. Schumacher doubled up with pain.

"Out of my way, damn you. Now open this door."

Schumacher moved awkwardly, limping. He opened the door.

"Tony, please—"

"You heard what I said. I'll get in touch with you. When I'm downstairs, throw this guy back out in the hall." Catell was at the stairs already.

"Tony! Tony, I'm sick!"

Catell was running down the stairs. He was whistling again. For a moment Schumacher staggered with a new rush of nausea that choked his throat and blurred his vision. Then, sweating with the effort, he dragged the limp agent back out into the hall. Panting and weak, Schumacher closed his eyes. When he looked at the man on the floor again, their eyes met. With a horrible effort the hurt agent strained his injured throat and let out a weird, loud scream.

As Schumacher staggered back into the room he could hear them clambering up the stairs. He was fumbling for his gun in the desk drawer. When they clattered up to the door, guns drawn, a rushing nausea curled Schumacher's insides. He lost sight of them, and with a head-splitting effort he retched helplessly. He heard noise, he heard the crash of the guns, and when he retched the second time, there was blood in the vomit.

They stepped up to him, dead in a mess on the floor, and they saw that he wasn't even holding the gun right.

At the corner of the street two men sat inside the closed truck among equipment and instruments. One sat at the short-wave radio; the other was fingering a Geiger counter. Suddenly the instrument crackled and ticked with a wild rush of discharges. Another ticker, standing nearby, did the same thing. The two men jumped.

"Christ Almighty, what in hell was that?"

Outside, a television repair truck turned the corner fast and lost itself in the traffic.

Chapter Four

The taxi wound slowly through the late-evening traffic. A thin spring rain had been drizzling all afternoon, almost like a fog, and the lights of downtown Detroit looked hazy. Catell and Selma sat in the cab, far apart on the back seat, not smiling.

"Hear the latest?" asked the cabby.

He didn't get an answer. Catell looked at Selma, who had wrapped a fox stole high around her neck, as if to protect herself from the thick dampness in the air.

"Did you hear the latest about the killing?" said the cabby, a little louder this time. He was a determined man.

"Answer the guy," Catell hissed. "Act natural."

"Uh, no, I haven't. What is the latest?" asked Selma.

"Remember reading about that killing in Highland Park a few days ago, where the cops shot a guy called Shoemaker? Well, they found out who the other guy was. The other guy who was in with old Shoemaker."

Catell tensed and leaned forward a little, his hands curled on the back of the driver's seat.

"Yeah?"

"Well, it turns out the other guy was a dame—beg pardon, a woman." The cabby let that sink in, waiting for some sound from the back.

"Oh, really?" Selma said at last.

"That's right. She was in the building all the time, disguised as a cleaning woman." The cabby paused significantly and then said in a triumphant voice, "And here is the pay-off: After the cops had went out, what does she do?"

"What?"

"She goes up to that Shoemaker's apartment, and she goes ahead and cleans up the mess there."

"She did? What mess?" Selma asked.

"The mess, you know. A guy gets shot up, there's a mess on the floor. Blood and so forth."

"That's terrible," Selma said.

"I'll say. Them molls are cold as ice when it comes to that kind of thing. Of course, she only did this to cover."

"Cover what?"

"To cover up her real purpose, that being the hidden goods."

"Oh, I see," Selma said. "What were those goods?"

"Well, they didn't say in the papers, but my wife knows the super's wife in that building. In other words, I have what might be called inside dope."

"And?"

"This friend of my wife's, the super's old lady, she figured Shoemaker for a suspicious character from way back. No visitors, no visible means of support, hardly ever went out—you know what I mean. Well, she'd go up to his place now and then, just to check. She'd look at the plumbing or the wallpaper, anything like that to check up on what was going on there. And what do you think she found?"

The cabby paused, but nobody said anything.

"She found stacks and stacks of road maps!"

"I don't understand," Selma said.

"Don't you get it? Road maps! Where do you get road maps, I ask you, except you walk in a filling station and ask for one? That's how he'd been collecting those road maps!"

The traffic got lighter on upper Woodward and the taxi

speeded up. Selma didn't say any more. She sat huddled in her corner of the seat, weary and withdrawn.

"So what was this moll picking up?" Catell asked.

"I'll tell you what she was picking up! Remember I was telling you about all them road maps? Do you also remember that slew of gas stations that got stuck up around Detroit and vicinity the last coupla months? Well, the guy what done it, he'd walk in the gas station, ask for a road map, and then stick the place up. Now, do you still want me to tell you what was stashed away in that apartment there?"

"Never mind," Catell said. "I can figure it. Schumach—I mean, Shoemaker had all the money from those gas-station holdups stashed up there, and his girl friend came to collect after he'd been shot, right?"

"You certainly are right," said the cabby with a sense of achievement.

Catell sat back in his seat. He pulled out a pack of cigarettes, lit one for himself, and then offered one to Selma. She shook her head and turned away.

How she remembered those road maps! Otto and she would sit on the couch nights and study the maps, talking about trips they'd take someday. Schumacher never took her on any of those trips, but he'd talk about them often, and Selma was sure he meant to take her away someday, to drive along the highways through different states, and to see all the points of interest that were marked on the maps. And Selma had liked the planning ahead; she had felt comfortable sitting on the couch there with old Otto.

"What's eating you?" Catell said.

"Nothing."

Selma bent her head so Catell couldn't see her eyes. She felt terribly alone and wished she could cry out, weep.

"Do something with your hair, kid. Those curls are coming down," Catell said.

"It's the damp, honey. I'm sorry."

"Well, fix it. We're almost there."

The taxi had swung off Woodward, out toward the country. A garish neon sign came closer, off to the right of the highway. It said, "Paar Excellence," first in red, then in pink, then in blue, and finally all together—red, pink, blue.

"Get happy, kid. Here we are." Catell straightened his tie.

The Paar Excellence had two sections. One was a road-house with name band, fried chicken, dancing, and drinks. The other was a private club. Freddie Paar ran both of them, and he probably even owned the place, though nobody knew for sure. In the roadhouse section he had a friendly nod for the patrons; in the club he knew every-body by name. He had to.

When Selma and Catell walked into the club entrance, a bruiser in a tuxedo asked for their cards.

"No cards," Catell said. "Just blew into town and haven't joined yet."

"No card, no enter," said the tuxedo.

"I been here before," Catell said.

"No card, no enter."

"Call Paar. Tell him Catell is here."

The tuxedo picked up a phone in the wall and talked into it. Then he hung up and said, "Wait here. He'll be right out."

They waited while the bruiser looked Catell up and down. He didn't give Selma a second look.

Then Paar came through the door that led to the club proper. He was short and his tuxedo was built around him like a piece of architecture. Above the upholstery in the shoulders his head looked small, even though his thinning black hair left him with a monstrous forehead.

"My dear Selma," he said, and kissed her hand. "And Tony, of course. Come in, come in."

They followed Paar through the door and into a dim, low room with a fireplace, a long bar, and scattered couches. A girl in black stockings and very little else took Selma's fur and Catell's overcoat. Then they took one of the couches while Paar sat opposite on a low coffee table.

"Well, Tony, what have you decided?"

"No business, Paar. We came on a social visit."

"Of course, Tony, and forgive me, Selma, but answer me just this, Tony. Am I your man, or do you do it directly?"

"Directly."

"Fine, Tony, fine. No hard feelings, you understand, but do call on me for any help, eh? And now I want you to have a drink on the house. I may join you later."

He smiled at both of them, patted Selma on the knee, and was gone. He did it all so smoothly that Catell felt like a clod. He saw that Selma was smiling at Paar's back, but he was in no mood for an argument.

A blonde waitress brought them their drinks. She was wearing a little apron that was attached to her body in some mysterious way. "On the house," she said. Catell didn't know whether he should smile back at her or not.

"What did he mean by that remark, is he your man or not?" Selma caught Catell in the middle of a thought.

"Huh?"

"Paar. What was he talking about?"

"Oh, nothing. About the heist. I talked with him about unloading something."

"So?"

"He was interested but I wasn't. He's too high."

"He knows what we got?"

"What *we* got?"

"Yeah, what *we* got! You weren't thinking of leaving me out of this, were you? You weren't thinking you could pay me off with rent money and an occasional date in a nightclub, were ya?"

Selma leaned her large face close to Catell and he could see the make-up and the pores of her skin. One of her curls was still hanging down and bobbed up and down like a spring when she talked.

"Calm down, damnit. We came here for a good time."

"So I'm asking again. Does he know what we got?"

"No, he doesn't know what *we* got. All he knows is there's a lot of it."

"So you said no to Paar. And how, big shot, are you gonna move the stuff we got, seeing you ain't too pleased with Paar?"

"Selma, for chrissakes, let's have a good time, huh?"

"How ya gonna move it?"

"All right. Stop yelling. I'm going to take it where Paar would take it. He let slip with something. Out on the West Coast."

"Where?"

"I don't know yet. I gotta make connections there first. L.A., probably."

Selma let herself sink back on the cushions of the couch. Catell could see where her corset pinched her and looked away.

"I love the sunshine. Gee, Tony, won't it be fun on the beach there and everything?"

"You want another drink?"

Selma didn't answer. She was looking up in the air,

smiling and saying "Gee" every so often. When the fresh drinks came, Catell took her hand.

"Honey, listen. Let's get one thing straight. This deal isn't through yet, and until it is, we gotta go easy. When Schumacher was around he staked me to some dough, but now there isn't any. Not till the deal comes through. So till then, we gotta go easy, not to speak of the risks. The way I figure it, you stay here and I do the scouting alone. Then I send for you. And then we can go anywhere you want. Whaddaya say?"

"But Tony!" Selma sounded hurt. "You mean that?"

"Just till I finish this business, honey. You know I can't be seen with you now They know you been a friend of Schumacher's, and I don't want to get connected to him in any way. It's too risky. Besides, I haven't got any dough right now."

"Tony, I got some. I got two thousand at home. I been saving it the longest time. And honest, Tony, I don't mind."

"It's no good, Selma. It's too risky for both of us. As long as I'm not connected with Schumacher in any way, everything is jake."

"Now you listen to me, Tony Catell. You better take care of me or else. Otto never would have acted that way. I'm going with you or else."

"Or else what?" Catell said it slowly and quietly, but Selma caught the tone.

"You don't scare me one bit, Tony Catell. If you think you can trample all over me and then walk out you got another guess coming. First you make me leave Otto, then you go get him shot to death so he's out of the way, and then you think you can just give me the boot and light out. Not on your life!"

"Selma, you're talking crazy. You got everything wrong. I never intended for Otto to end up that way."

"Oh, yes, you did, lovin' cup. I know your kind, but it ain't gonna happen to me." Selma gave Catell an ugly look and drained her glass. "I want another drink, right now. And don't tell me you're broke, lovin' cup."

Catell controlled his temper and waved for another drink.

"And from now on, any plans you got you discuss with me, lovin' cup, understand? I been around long enough to know how to handle your kind."

"That's for sure."

"What's that? And another thing. I want you to know I despise you from the bottom of my heart, lovin' cup, for what you did to my Otto. That was the lowest, swiniest—"

"Stop calling me loving cup."

Selma stopped in the middle of her sentence and looked vacantly at Catell. Then suddenly she buried her face in the palms of her hands and started to cry. She bawled with a wet and cowlike sound, crying, "Lovin' cup!" between hiccups.

"My dear, my dear, my dear!"

Paar had reappeared from somewhere and he was patting Selma on the back and stroking her bare arm.

"Beat it, Paar. She'll be all right." Catell felt uncomfortable.

"My good Tony, you don't seem to know how a lady likes to be treated at a time like this. One moment, Tony. You are my guests here, so allow me to help you with this little matter. Why don't you go and buy some cigarettes, and when you come back, everything will be all right. Won't it, Selma dear?" He put his hand on Selma's shoulder.

Catell got up and looked around the room. Let that bald monkey handle that mess and her sloppy curls. Live and let live, he thought. How that lousy bag got him to make a pitch for her he didn't know. Catell walked to the bar and ordered a shot. Back on the couch he saw Paar sitting next to Selma, who was patting her eyes and nodding her head. If Paar thought he was getting a deal there, he had a big, mushy surprise coming. And welcome to it.

Catell let his eyes wander over the dim room. Couples were sitting or standing together, there were groups of young punks in tuxedos, and everybody looked prosperous. Catell recognized one or two faces; the rest were strangers to him. Everybody was young, slick-looking, and everybody seemed very sure of himself. Then Catell thought of California. Pretty soon now he would be back on top. In a very short time all these punks were going to hear about Tony Catell.

"Where do I get smokes in this place?" he asked the bartender.

The guy nodded to the left and kept on wiping a glass. Catell was going to say something else, but his eyes had followed the direction of the nod. He saw a young blonde with long wavy hair who was carrying a cigarette tray in front of her. She was dressed in a brief thing like a corset, all black, and the rest of her was the most satiny, fair thing he had ever seen. The girl had the improbable figure of a calendar nude, and most of it showed. She turned around and came his way. She walked with a high-heeled bounce that made her breasts move. They were full, and Catell noticed that the black corset just made it in front.

He asked for cigarettes and she took a pack from her tray. Then she tore the pack open, shook out a cigarette, and offered it to him. He stuck the cigarette in his mouth and she gave him a light from a small gold lighter she carried. Over the cigarette Catell caught the girl's eye. She looked at him in an unconcerned way, smiling with the corners of her mouth. Then his eyes wandered down again.

"Don't you want them, sir?"

"What's that?"

"Your cigarettes, sir. Don't you want them?"

He grabbed the pack out of her hand and gave her a bill. She smiled her thanks and slowly moved down the aisle in front of the bar. Catell could have sworn that she didn't know he was staring at her.

He walked back to the couch where Paar was sitting next to Selma. She was smiling again, looking pretty good in the dim light. Paar's hand was lying on her thigh. When Catell walked up Paar moved his hand away slowly, as if he didn't care one way or the other.

"I see you got some cigarettes," he said.

"Yeah."

"I think I fixed your little quarrel very nicely, Tony, my boy. Selma is in a very good mood again and I don't want you to spoil it for her."

"Yeah?"

"He won't," Selma said, smiling at Paar. "He's really a nice boy, aren't you, lovin' cup?" She had a brassy smile on her big face. " 'Scuse me, gents, while I do a little fixing." She got out of the couch with an effort.

"Sit down, Catell, sit down. Selma and I have become great friends while you were gone. She tells me you're leaving us. You have other interests, maybe?"

Ignoring Paar's question, Catell jerked his head toward the blonde cigarette girl. "Who is she?"

"Selma is a little upset about your plans. Or at least she

was before she and I had our little talk. We both feel you should stick around, Tony."

"What's in it for me?"

"She's only eighteen, Tony. Besides, she's been spoken for. However, as I was saying—"

"We got no business, Paar. I told you I'll only deal direct."

"As you wish, Tony. But let me remind you, Selma is a very emotional woman. Ah, did you know that our little Lily is leaving us?"

"Who?"

"Lily. The young thing you've been admiring so. And as I've said, she's been spoken for, Tony. She's leaving for Los Angeles."

"So what?"

"I think Selma mentioned something about your going to Los Angeles, or am I mistaken? Of course, Selma doesn't know that Lily is going to Los Angeles, Tony."

"And what if she does? What exactly are you trying to pull?"

"Just this, Catell: I think you might do better staying here. And, I repeat, if there is any way in which I can be of help to you—"

"Can it. Here's Selma."

When she sat down on the couch, Paar rose and turned to go.

"Don't leave now, Paar honey," said Selma, grabbing his sleeve. "Sit down for a minute and we'll talk some more. With Tony here," and she gave Catell a cocky smile.

"Later, dear Selma. We'll all have a nice chat, I promise you." Paar wasn't smiling this time.

"Paar." Catell's voice was matter of fact. "Who are the two guys just came in the door?"

"Who?"

"Don't jerk your head. By the door."

Paar turned and glanced toward the entrance. Then he gave Catell a patronizing smile.

"You are jumpy, Tony. They come quite often. Local detectives looking in on a private club."

Catell rose slowly. He put his hands in his pockets, turned his back to the cops, and looked casual.

"I'm blowing. Where's the back door?"

"My dear Tony, this means absolutely nothing. Please sit down."

"Shut up. I can't be seen with Selma right now. Where's the back?"

"Now, really, Tony boy." Paar put his soft hand on Catell's arm.

Catell stepped close. "Hear this, Paar. See to it I don't tangle with your copper friends there. Keep them and anybody else you know out of my way. If you don't, I'll get you."

Then he walked away, slowly, without turning. Paar's big forehead was sticky with sweat.

Once through the swinging doors in the back, Catell turned quickly and glanced through the glass into the room he had just left. Paar was standing with the two cops, patting one of them on the back. Then they started to walk his way, chatting.

Catell turned away. He found himself in an empty kitchen with one light over the huge refrigerator. There was a door to the left. Catell went to the door, opened it, and stepped into a long hall. More doors. He picked one, opened it, and found himself in a small cubicle without windows. Pipes ran along the ceiling. There was a mop and bucket in one corner, and a clothes rack in the other.

A naked light bulb made a hard light, and under it stood Lily.

She had taken her shoes and stockings off and her hands were at her back, trying to undo the black corset. Catell closed the door behind him and she looked up, without recognition. "Hi," Catell said.

"Hi."

"Fancy meeting you here, Lily." She didn't answer. Only her eyes moved. "If you were going to scream, don't," Catell said. He turned the catch of the door. "I'm just staying a minute." She looked at him, frowning, and put a hand to her breasts. "Please," she said. "Please leave."

Catell heard footsteps in the hall and leaned lightly against the door, both hands on the knob. "Not a word, kid."

"Please, mister, I—"

Catell moved across the small room fast and clapped one hand over her mouth, holding her up against him with his other arm. He didn't have to say any more. She saw his face grow stiff, mean, and she stayed very still.

After the footsteps had passed, Catell didn't move right away. He felt her soft mouth under his hand and the curve of her thighs against him. Then he let her go. She stepped back, red marks showing on her face where his hand had been.

"Please go now."

"Not yet."

"Please, I have to change. I'm late."

"Go ahead."

"But I have to change, mister."

"The name's Tony."

She bit her lip but didn't say anything. One of the pipes along the ceiling started to hiss. Lily looked up and back at Catell, who was still leaning against the door. Neither of them moved.

"Come on, go ahead and change. Don't tell me you never been looked at."

She stood in the middle of the bare room, under the hard light, her mouth trembling.

"Answer me," Catell said.

"I—I don't know what you mean."

"I said get undressed. It can't be the first time."

"I never—"

"You're lying."

"Never like this, I mean."

"Fine. I like to be the first. Now get it off."

She hesitated. He took a step toward her, looking at the girl with cold eyes. A muscle jumped in the side of his face. Lily shrank back, real fear in her eyes.

"Stay where you are. Under the light."

Catell leaned against the door again and watched.

Lily arched her back, her hands fumbling for the zipper. Her eyes shone wet. When the zipper opened she let the corset drop. It rolled on the floor without losing its shape. Then Catell raised his eyes slowly. He saw her narrow ankles, her calves. She had full thighs that curved with a satiny sheen, wide round hips, and a sharp curve where her waist drew in. Catell chewed his lip but otherwise made no movement. He noticed that she had the same shape as she'd had in the corset, the skin of her body smooth and unmarked from the stays, and her breasts high. They were ripe, coming to impudent points, and they threw sharp shadows, which moved with her breathing. He looked at her face. She was very young.

"Turn around."

She turned slowly, looking at him over her shoulder. "Now lie down."

She lay down on the cold cement floor, legs drawn up. "Stretch out."

She did. She pointed her toes, legs together, and put her arms over her head. All the while she looked at him with large eyes. Catell never moved from his place by the door. After a while he told her to get up. He walked over to her and brushed the lint from her naked back. Then he went back to the door.

"You can get dressed now, Lily."

While she put her clothes on, Catell lit another cigarette and smoked without looking at her.

"May I go now?" Lily had stepped close to the door.

"Sure."

He opened the door for her and let her pass. Just as she went by he grasped her arm and said, "I'm the first? Right, Lily?"

"Yes, mister."

"Tony."

"Yes, Tony."

Their eyes held for a moment. Catell frowned.

"You're a hard one."

She started to smile, gave it up. "No," she said.

Catell closed the door again. Lily waited.

"So why'd you do it, just like that?"

"I didn't, just like that."

"Why'd you do it?"

This time her small smile didn't make it at all. "It didn't hurt," she said.

"What does?"

She smiled a moment. "Not much," she said, and looked down at her feet.

"Lily."

"Yes?"

"Your folks in L.A.?"

"I don't think so," she said. She said it in no special way, and that's what gave it the meaning.

Catell didn't ask any more. He opened the door, stepped back. When he put his hand on her arm again it surprised both of them.

"Lily."

"Yes, Tony?"

"See you?"

"I'd like to," she said.

She finished saying it and then went out. He closed the door behind her.

When he had smoked his cigarette he crushed it under his foot and walked back the way he had come. He didn't see the two detectives, but Paar was standing by the swinging doors.

"You may come out now, Tony." Paar smiled.

"They gone?"

"Yes. In fact, quite a while ago. And furthermore, I'm afraid you will have to go home alone. Selma has left, too. They took her."

"What are you talking about?"

"The detectives. They took her along for routine questioning about old Schumacher, it seems."

Catell didn't answer right away.

"Lily gone too?" He didn't look at Paar.

"Why, yes, Tony. She had to make an early plane. L.A., you know. I think I mentioned it."

"You did."

"I didn't mention, though, who she's going to join. I don't know if you've ever heard of him, but his name is Topper. And if I were you, Tony, I'd stay away from Topper."

Catell left Paar standing there. He got his coat and took a taxi back to town. He left Detroit that same night, but first he stopped at Selma's apartment and took the two thousand bucks that was there.

Chapter Five

Paar didn't like Catell very much. He didn't understand him, and he didn't have any patience with his kind. But Paar didn't want Catell to come to any harm. Not yet, anyway.

After Catell had left the club, Paar walked slowly toward the bar, then changed his mind and went to his office. He closed the heavy door, took off his dinner jacket, and sat down behind his desk. Without his padding Paar looked narrow and stoop-shouldered. He put his hands on the large desktop and frowned. It would be very nice to let the cops pump Selma dry. The drunken slut would implicate herself and get locked out of the way. She would spill what it was Catell had hidden and Paar had enough pull to find out whatever the cops might get out of her. And finally they'd find out for sure whether she knew where Catell was going from here. If she didn't know, then Paar would be happy to know that he didn't have to bother with her. If she did know, the cops would get to him first, and Paar wouldn't have a chance. The thought pained him, but he'd have to take Selma on himself.

Paar sighed, picked up the phone, and dialed a city number. A butler answered at the other end.

"Let me talk to him," said Paar.

The butler knew Paar's voice and said, "One moment, sir."

Then a voice said, "What is it, Paar?"

"Two dicks hauled in a friend of mine, a woman. She'll be at the Fifth Precinct house for questioning. Get her out....I know it's two o'clock in the morning, but I want her out....No, just questioning. No warrant....I'll be over there in half an hour to pick her up, so do what you have to do. She was picked up at my club. The men's names are Porter and Levy. So long."

Paar put down the phone, took his jacket and overcoat, and left the club. Twenty minutes later his chauffeur-driven limousine stopped in front of the Fifth Precinct police station. Paar entered the building with an affable smile for everyone; two drunks, one plainclothesman, and the desk sergeant. Paar leaned his elbow on the high desk and offered the policeman a cigarette.

"No, thank you, Mr. Paar. We haven't seen you in a long time."

"That's true, Sergeant Stone." Paar smiled at him. "Is the young lady ready?"

"I'm very sorry, Mr., Paar, they're still questioning her."

Paar's neck got red and his voice didn't sound polite. "Didn't you get a call to release her?"

"Sure, Mr. Paar, but—"

"Well?"

The Sergeant leaned on his desk and lowered his voice. "Don't try and throw your weight around, Paar. The Feds are in on this. They're with her now."

For a moment Paar was stunned. He recovered himself with an effort and asked, "What room?"

"Two-o-five."

He went to the second floor and walked through the door of 205 without knocking. What he saw made him blanch. Four men were sitting around the figure by the table. It was Selma, head back, mouth open, eyes closed. One arm hung down limp.

"Who are you?" They turned around and looked at him.

"Come here," said another one.

Paar stepped closer, staring at Selma. One of the four men leaned over from his chair and grabbed Paar.

"Under the light, Bud. Let's take a look at you."

Paar's big forehead glistened and his berry eyes blinked. "Gentlemen, please. What—what have you done?"

"This is Freddie Paar, friends," said one of the men. He was a detective out of the Fifth Precinct. The others were FBI.

"Freddie Paar is our local glamour boy of the dark, dark underworld. Name any smutty business, Paar is in it. Right, boy?" The man laughed.

With an effort Paar straightened his back. "I came to fetch this young lady and they sent me to this room. However, this shocking scene—"

"This shocking scene!" the detective said, and laughed. Paar turned to him with a face like poison. "I'm not without influence in this town. This outrage—"

"This outrage!" aped the man, and he doubled over with laughter.

"There are laws," Paar said, his voice getting shrill. "Clubbing women into unconsciousness—"

At that point Selma began to snore. "Unconsciousness!" the man roared.

This made Selma start. She woke with a sick face, licking her dry lips.

"Selma," Parr said. "What have they done to you?"

"Lovin' cup." Her voice was raspy.

The detective stopped laughing and got serious. "Lovin' cup," he said to Paar, "your friend here was drunk when she came in. She fell asleep."

"You mean she hasn't been questioned yet?"

A quiet voice from the end of the room said, "No."

Herron stepped forward and looked at Paar. "And what is your interest in this matter, may I ask?"

"The young lady is a personal acquaintance, sir. She spent the evening at my club, and when I saw her leave with two detectives, naturally I got concerned and made inquiries."

"With whom did she spend the evening?" Herron asked.

"I don't know. Some young man or other."

"Where is he?"

"I couldn't tell you that, sir."

"I think we'll throw you out now, lovin' cup," said the detective. "Shall I throw him out, Herron?"

"No. Mr. Paar may stay. As soon as his lady friend has recovered, he'll want to take her home, I'm sure."

Paar was very anxious to take Selma home. He didn't like Herron. Polite cops made him uncomfortable and Herron smelled like FBI.

"Selma, are you ready to leave?"

"Oh, Jaysis," she said, holding her head.

"Did they annoy you, Selma? Question you?"

"Jaysis."

Paar couldn't make anything of that remark and it upset him. He straightened himself and looked at Herron. "I demand an explanation. What is this lady doing here?"

"She is suffering from a hangover," the detective said.

"And we wanted some information from her about an acquaintance of hers," Herron added.

"Well, you must realize by now that you're wasting your time," Paar said. "If I can be of any assistance—"

"No, thank you, Mr. Paar. Our information is complete, for the moment."

"If you're wondering about her escort, Mr. Catell has left town New York, I think."

Herron shifted his head slightly and the man next to

him made notes on a stenographer's pad in front of him.

"You didn't know this?" said Paar, who had noticed the movement.

"No. We were actually interested in one Otto Schumacher."

Paar cursed himself under his breath. Now they had Catell tagged and Paar himself had done the damage. He smiled nervously.

"Well, it's of no consequence. And as I was saying, Mr. Catell was here only briefly. He mentioned to me how anxious he was to get back to New York. In fact, I believe he took the one-o'clock train."

Herron made no comment. The stenographer was sharpening his pencil, the detective stood near the wall picking his teeth, and the fourth man was holding a paper cup of water to Selma's lips.

"Oh, Jaysis!" she said.

The silence made Paar uncomfortable. He still didn't know whether they had got anything out of Selma.

"If you gentlemen are through, I believe I'll accompany the lady home now." Paar took Selma by the arm.

"Of course, Mr. Paar. We'll be in touch with her. And you," Herron added.

Paar helped Selma out of the chair. One shoulder of her deep-cut dress was slipping down her arm and her left stocking sagged She looked terrible. Outside, even the cold night air didn't seem to help her. Selma sat in one corner of Paar's big limousine, never saying a word. Nor did Paar. It could wait till morning, he figured. He and Selma were going to stick together for a while, seeing they were both after the same man. Meanwhile, there'd be some compensations, and he looked at Selma's inert figure leaning in the corner of the seat.

"End of the line," Paar said in a cheery voice. It didn't cheer Selma.

"Jaysis," she said.

He helped her out of the car and into the apartment building. They went up in the elevator. Once in the apartment, Paar locked the door.

"Selma, dear, sit down and be comfortable. Your wrap, oops, thank you. And now, sweet, the hair of the dog for you."

Selma straightened up and patted her hair. She looked more animated now and struck a saucy pose. The dress had slipped off one shoulder again.

Paar sat down next to Selma and handed her a glass of straight whisky. She drank it fast, wrinkling her eyes at him over the rim of the glass.

"Paar, baby, you're a lover." She put a whisky-wet kiss on his big forehead.

"How would you know?" Paar said. He patted her shoulder. "But it's good to see you cheered up again, Selma. Your ordeal at the station—"

"One more, Paar baby." She handed him her empty glass.

"Did they question you long, dear?" Paar refilled Selma's glass and held it just out of reach.

"Come on, baby, come on." He gave her the glass quickly, noticing how easily she could lose her temper. After two swallows Selma put the glass down and leaned back, sighing. "Paar, you're so good to me."

"Don't mention it, my dear. And stay as long as you like. In fact, Selma, what do you say you move in with me? The place is large, I'm alone, I could use an attractive hostess when I entertain."

Selma wasn't answering. Her face was flushed now

and she was staring at the ceiling with a vague smile.

"Selma, my dear, are you all right?"

"Jaysis."

Paar saw it was no use. She didn't resist when he pulled her up and steered her toward the bedroom. He hadn't expected she would. Sitting on the large bed, Selma smiled pleasantly when Paar started to unbutton her dress.

"You'll be comfortable soon now." His hands were sweating. "We'll talk about Catell in the morning, sweetness. And you'll tell me all about your bad, bad time with the police."

He took her dress off, Selma lifting her rear so he could pull it up. Sitting down again, she swayed a little, eyes closed. Paar steadied her and started to fumble with her brassiere.

"Soon now, my dearest, soon you'll be all right, eh, Selma?" He got the brassiere unhooked and pulled the straps off her shoulders. His voice was shaky when he said, "Darling."

Selma sank back on the bed, sighing. With nervous movements Paar fumbled with his dinner jacket while he ran to the light switch. He was pulling his tie off when he clicked the light switch.

Out of the darkness Selma said, "Jaysis."

Chapter Six

"Why'd you let 'em go?" The detective was still picking his teeth.

"I got all the information I need at the moment," Herron said. He was shuffling through the stenographer's notes,

"Coffee, anyone?" The fourth man stuck his head in the door.

"Not for me." Herron lit himself a cigarette and shuffled through the notes again.

"Bring me one, Charlie, black," the detective said.

The detective walked from the door to the window, looked down into the dark street, and walked back again. "I got all night yet," he said.

"Yeah?"

He walked again. The stenographer had put his overcoat on and gone out.

"What you learn, Jack?" the detective asked. He spat out a little piece of toothpick and sat down opposite Herron.

"Well, for one thing, that Catell didn't go to New York."

"Yeah, that Paar sure was anxious for you to think so."

"Where's the phone?"

"Next room. Wish Charlie'd hurry up with that coffee."

Herron went next door and dialed a number. "Hello? Herron here. Who's on duty?...O.K., give me Agent Polnik." Herron waited, scribbling in his notebook. "Polnik? Listen. Have somebody check if there was a train for

New York at one A.M. Get the New York office to have a man wait for the train, if there was one....What? Not till five A.M.? O.K., then skip that angle. Now, listen. We're looking for Anthony Catell. Look him up in the file I left in the office....Yes, one of the files I got there. Next, cover the station, airport, bus terminals for the next twenty-four hours....Yes, same man. Pay special attention to anything leaving for Los Angeles....No, I'm not sure. We have one informant to go by, but she was drunk. But Catell might fit into the picture because of other information....Uh-huh, he knew Schumacher. One more thing, and this is important. Have the men carry Geiger counters. And check baggage rooms....Yeah. O.K., 'bye."

Herron hung up and went back to the other room. The detective was drinking black coffee and chewing a fresh toothpick. Charlie was spooning a milk shake out of a paper carton.

"How you can eat that stuff is beyond me," the detective was saying.

"Makes more sense than eating toothpicks."

"Well, Jack, what next?" The detective looked up when Herron came in.

"We're covering the usual. Probably useless. Catell is no greenhorn. Lemme have a sip." Herron took the coffee cup and drank.

"Whyn't you buy one? Charlie asked you if you wanted one."

"I don't want a whole cup, just a sip. Coffee keeps me awake."

"So let's have my cup back."

Herron stacked his notes together and got up to leave. "Does Paar have any connections in L.A.?"

"Yeah," Charlie said. "Some syndicate tie-up. You can find out downstairs."

"O.K., I will. Anybody here to take the teletype?"

"Try three doors down the hall, you can't miss the racket."

"Thanks. Night, all."

"Night."

"Lucky bastard."

Three doors down Herron dictated his message. In St. Louis, Chief Jones watched the teletype as it hammered out: "Herron to Jones. Circumstantial evidence of association with deceased O. Schumacher and former girlfriend of same make T. Catell definite suspect. Screening of Detroit exits ordered. No present trace of stolen object. Presumably in suspect's possession. Am proceeding Los Angeles via plane to cover suspect's connections and possible arrival there. Details follow. Communicate L.A. district office."

At ten-thirty-five A.M. the next day, Herron boarded a through plane to Los Angeles. He arrived late that evening, checked into the district office, then got himself a hotel room. He slept for nine hours and then went back to work. He checked leads, covered angles, made reports, waited. He did this for days without finding a trace of Tony Catell.

On a hot stretch of road in Arizona, Catell stopped the car and wiped the sweat off his neck. He listened to the gurgling of the radiator, watching the steam hiss out from under the hood. He pulled out a cigarette. Before he got it lit the thought of the smoke made him feel sick and he threw the thing away. He got out of the car. For a moment he fought nausea that rose in his throat like wet cotton. The feeling passed.

It had started a few days after he'd left Detroit, and now it came every day, at odd times, first a vague dizziness,

later sick waves of nausea and knots of pain, till the car
would swerve and he'd pull himself together again. Then
it would pass away. Sometimes he wondered whether
Schumacher had been right about the gold. He'd called it
rotten. But there was a better reason. Catell looked at his
watch and pulled a sticky candy bar out of his pocket.
Two o'clock. Time.

Every two hours Catell ate a candy bar, whether he
was hungry or not. By the time he reached Los Angeles
he would have gained ten, fifteen pounds, maybe. Already
he looked like a different man, with more bulk, the lines
of his face less deep. He had a tan, and his hair, black and
straight, was getting longer.

When the car had stopped sizzling, Catell walked
around to the front and lifted the hood.

"Troubles, Buddy?"

Catell jumped around and saw the police car. A lean
man in uniform and cowboy hat looked at him.

"Jumpy, ain't ya?"

"I didn't hear you come up."

"Stranger here, ain't ya?" The man climbed out of his
car and stretched his long legs. There was a sheriff's badge
on his blue shirt. "I said, you must be a stranger here,
huh?"

Catell didn't like the man. Not just because he was a
cop, but because there was that grinning curiosity on his
face, that eager prying of a lean dog scurrying around to
find something, anything. The man stuck his neck out,
red and wrinkled like a turkey's, and spat.

"Speak up, stranger."

"Yeah. I'm a stranger here."

"Where from?"

"Look at the license."

The sheriff looked without wanting to. It said Louisiana.

"I'm asking you."

"New Orleans."

"City fella, huh?" He stalked around the car and kicked at the loose fender in the rear. "You drive this junker all the way up from the Gulf?"

"Sure. And don't kick it again."

The man just laughed. "You know, city feller, we got an ordinance about junkers. We like people comin' through here to drive a safe car. Don't want folks around here to get endangered."

"So stop kicking at it, hear?" Catell's voice shook with rage and he suddenly felt cold under his wet shirt. That bastard was getting to him.

"How about pullin' that heap off the pavement some more, city feller? We got an ordinance about highway parking."

Catell got behind the wheel and kicked at the starter. The gears crashed and the car jumped ahead a few feet, off the paved strip of highway. That bastard, that lousy hick bastard. Catell took a deep breath. What he could do to that raw-necked, rat-faced— Better not think like this. Better think of the big things at stake here, better look like you're taking it. Got to take it.

"One more thing, city feller. Don't park where you're parkin' there. We got an ordinance." He laughed, his Adam's apple bobbing. He jumped back in his car and pulled it up even with Catell's.

"I'll be by after a spell. Better not be here no more." He shot away, the wheels spitting gravel at Catell's windshield.

After a few minutes Catell got out of the car again and slammed the hood shut. It made a nasty sound and some-

thing came loose, leaving the hood jammed at an angle.
The damn car was corning apart at the seams. First he'd
had a pretty good one, but it had Michigan license plates
and the car had to be ditched. He hid it in a ravine somewhere in Indiana and buried the license plates. Then he
hitchhiked for a hundred miles. Next he bought a prewar
job in southern Indiana and drove it as far as Kentucky.
That's where he drove it into an abandoned mine after
throwing away the plates. At night he walked to the
nearest town, took a train for two hundred miles, and
then bought the third car. He drove it to Terryville, Louisiana, left it in a vacant lot, and bought his last car. This
was a real junker, but there wasn't much choice. Selma's
two thousand was almost gone.

Catell started the car and headed it back on the hot
pavement. There better be a town close by. The radiator
was almost empty and there probably wasn't much oil
left. The old car gathered speed, whining down the white
road and shooting thick black clouds out the tailpipe.

A sign flipped by, saying: "You are entering—" and it
was gone. After a bend in the road a tree appeared, two
trees; then Catell saw the houses. They were gray clap-
board and looked old. Some were adobe. The only new-
looking place was the filling station, rigged up like a fort,
and Catell breathed easier.

When he pulled up to the pumps he heard the gravel
crunch on the right. A car stopped sharply and the voice
said, "City feller, don't they got not ordinance about
speeding where you come from?"

The sheriff got out of his car and grinned, crackly lips
drawn back over his gums.

"Get out," he said.

"What in hell do you want now?"

"Don't get porky, stranger. I'm the law around here and you just broke one of our ordinances."

"What goddamn ordinance?"

"The one about speedin'. You gonna pay up or you gonna spend some time in our jail?"

"How much will you take, *officer?*"

"Seeing it's you, city feller, that'll be seventy dollars."

"Why, you stinking sonofabitch!" Catell jumped out of his car. His door hit the gas pump and slammed back into his chest. Before he could get free, the sheriff had come around the car, swinging a sap that came down hard and caught Catell on the shoulder. But the sheriff was slow; too slow for Catell, anyway. Twisting his injured shoulder back, Catell lashed out with one foot and caught the tall man in the groin. Before he had time to double over and groan, Catell's hand caught the back of his neck and jerked it down, and a knee smashed up into the sheriff's face. Then a sharp kick into the chest and the half-conscious man flew back, crashing hard into a pump. There wasn't any time for Catell to enjoy the sight because a sharp blow from behind made him buckle and pitch, and then all turned black.

"I guess they both ain't gonna be much for a while," said the thickset man who was holding a two-by-four in his hand.

"Reckon," said the short one next to him. "What'll we do now?"

"To the jailhouse. The stranger here has some explainin' to do, and Harry—well, Harry just natcherly belongs in the jailhouse, seein' he's our sheriff." They both laughed.

"Sure makes me feel good, seein' our Harry get his for

a change. Had it comin' for a long time," said the short one. "I just feel kinda sorry for that stranger here, once Harry starts feelin' like himself again."

They laughed again and then started to drag the two limp figures over the gravel.

Chapter Seven

A bottle fly kept buzzing around the cell. It hit the walls with a small flat sound. Every time it hit, fine yellow dust sifted down from the adobe. A few times it made for the light that came through the barred window, but even though there was no glass, the fly didn't find its way out. Then it angled down into the shadow, hit the wall again, and landed on Catell's face. It sat there for a long tune without Catell's knowing it. When he came to, he did so with a start, slapping his hand over his forehead with a wide awkward swing. He jumped up, but weaved and doubled over. There was a blue ache in his left shoulder, and the pain in his head made red fire flash before his eyes.

After a moment he straightened up. His eyes ran over the adobe walls, the barred hole of a window, and the bars that made one wall of his cell. There was a room beyond, but Catell didn't take it in because closer by, near the iron door, the sheriff sat hunched on a three-legged stool. His eyes and nose were puffed with a purple shimmer, and his lips were curled back, showing his long yellow teeth. Three teeth in front were missing, and his tongue was probing back and forth over the reddened hole.

"Sleep good, city feller?" He talked with a hiss. Catell walked up to the bars but didn't answer.

"I'm askin' because for a spell now that's goin' to be your last good sleep."

The sheriff got up slowly and walked to a desk near the door beyond. He came back with a pencil and pad. After sitting down again he said, "What's your name, stranger?"

"Jesse Weiss."

"Age?"

"Forty-eight."

"Where from?"

"New Orleans."

The questions went on and Catell gave answers. He kept his voice even and his eyes down. There were going to be no more mistakes. In the time of a minute he had made all the bad ones: attracting attention, resisting arrest, assaulting an officer of the law, landing in jail. No more mistakes now. Don't offend the man; do what he says; act small and a little scared. And wait for the breaks. This wasn't the end. This was bad, but not the end. For God's sake, this was not the end!

"Now listen close, city feller, because I want you to know what I got in mind. Like I tried to tell you once before, I'm the law around here, and you went ahead and broke that law more'n a couple of times. Now we can't have that around here, city feller. You gotta learn how to stay on the right side of the law."

Catell had his hands around the bars, listening with eyes down, when the sheriff stopped talking. Catell looked up and caught the blurred movement too late. The sap smacked down sharply, cracking across the back of his right hand.

"You listening to me, New Orleans? You paying attention to what I say?"

Catell didn't hear him. He had jerked back, gasping with the pain that exploded in his hand. His knees buckled and he groaned hoarsely, his good hand tightening around the wrist of the other arm. The sheriff had got off his chair, watching. His tongue was working the hole in his gums like a lazy snake.

"That's just so you know who to pay attention to around here, New Orleans. Now, like I was saying, you gotta learn to respect the law, and I'm just the man what can teach you how."

Catell sat on the floor, his breath making a harsh labored sound. The hand was puffing up fast.

"So I figure the best way of doing that, city feller, is for you to stay around here a little while. Then, when I see some real improvement, why, then we'll start figuring on some kind of trial for you. The judge at the county seat is a friend of mine, so we'll see what can be done in the case of the Law versus City Feller. Any questions? No? I didn't figure so."

The sheriff stood a while looking at Catell on the floor. Then he started to laugh. He laughed with a slow babbling sound that could have meant anything.

"I'm going to leave you for a spell now, seeing you'd rather be alone with your little aches and pains. And in case you crave company, there's a deputy right beyond that door, sittin' on the porch."

The sheriff turned away and left, still shaking with his slow gobble of a laugh.

Catell stayed on the floor for a while, watching his hand. The swelling was dark red now, but the pain wasn't so unbearable any more. Except when he moved his fingers.

Alone in the jailhouse, Catell started to look around. Standing at the bars, he could glimpse a cell on either side of him. There was a door to the left, half open, with a toilet visible. Beyond the corridor was the long room that served as an office. Through the two windows Catell could see a porch and a country street.

The bars of the window in his cell were solid. So were the ones that formed one wall of his cell. But the lock of the cell was nothing. A strong nail, bent, or perhaps a spoon, he thought, any simple thing like that would do it. Tonight? Tomorrow. Sitting down carefully on the cot, Catell thought about it. Why rush? That bastard hick of a sheriff wasn't in any hurry to move to court. So wait. Wait for the breaks. And the longer the sheriff waited, the more he would get in the wrong. And the more he got in the wrong, the less of a leg he'd have to stand on. Catell felt better.

Suddenly he jumped up, fright in his eyes. The gold! Where was his car? In panicky confusion he ran to the bars, shaking them, rattling the door. He curled the fingers of his injured hand, not feeling the pain, with only one thought in his mind. The gold! Then he ran to the window, to shake the bars, to reach his arm far out of the yellow hole that faced nothing but hot dust and weeds. Then he saw it. His car was standing in back of the jail. One door was half open and nothing looked any different about the car than when he had bought it. He could see the back seat, undisturbed. Draped over the seat was the lead apron.

With a deep breath Catell stepped back from the window and sank down on his cot. He was tired. He stretched out carefully, with one arm over his eyes, the injured hand resting on his stomach. The dull heat of the cell lay like lead around him, but Catell hardly noticed it. He slept.

°

"Just look at him sweat," said the deputy to the three ranchers. They stood outside the cell, watching Catell asleep on his cot.

"You think he's sweating now, boys, just wait till I get through with him," said the sheriff. "Ben, get me a bucket of water."

The deputy went outside and came back with the bucket. "Whatcha gonna do, Harry?"

"Just step back and watch."

Heaving the bucket in a wide arc, the sheriff tossed the water at Catell. It caught him full on the neck and face. The sleeping man jerked up with a wild gasp, dumb bewilderment in his face. There was a roar of laughter from the men who were peering through the bars, with stamping of feet and back-slapping.

"What's his name?" one of them asked.

"Call him New Orleans," said the sheriff. "He likes to be called New Orleans. It makes him think of the big city. Right, New Orleans?"

Catell stood up slowly but didn't answer.

"He don't answer," said another rancher, and they all looked at the sheriff. "Harry, he don't answer."

"He will." The sheriff pushed the men aside and stepped up to the door. He pulled out a large key and swung the door open. In the silence there was only the creak of the old floor and a soft swish as the sheriff unholstered his gun. Leveling the long revolver at Catell, he stood back with feet wide apart.

"Come out."

They all stood still, waiting.

"Come out, city feller."

Catell stepped forward slowly. His head was down and water dripped from his hair.

"Walk to that door."

Catell walked. He walked out of his cell, past the staring men, past the sheriff with his gun. Suddenly the sheriff kicked out his foot and Catell was flung to the floor. Shaking his wet head, he heard the guffaws of the men behind him.

"It don't pay being hasty, New Orleans." The sheriff roared again. "Lemme give you a hand."

Catell obeyed.

"The other hand, city feller."

He reached up his swollen hand automatically but jerked it back, afraid of the pain.

"Your hand, city feller."

Catell shrank back when the sheriff's foot caught him under the chin. His head snapped back and hit the floor with a sharp thump. He lay limp and unconscious.

The sheriff doubled over with loud, dry laughter, slapping his thigh.

"Hey, New Orleans!" Then he noticed that he laughed alone. The young deputy stood by, snickering; the ranchers looked embarrassed.

"We'll be goin' now, Harry. We got things to do."

"Sure, Harry. We'll be seeing you. So long, Harry."

They looked away and hurried out. They didn't look at Harry, or at the limp wet man on the floor, and they closed the door softly behind them.

The sheriff holstered his gun and gave the young deputy a mean look.

"Throw him in the cell. And mind, you stay around an' keep an eye on him. He bears watching." Then he walked out, hitting the floor hard with his heels.

*

When it was getting dark outside, Catell woke up. He breathed carefully, feeling the aches in his body. He heard dim voices from the porch. The door opened and the sheriff came in, followed by a few other men. Catell stiffened. This time, he swore, this time he'd kill the bastard, no matter what the consequences. But they didn't come his way. They stood talking in the front room and only the sheriff gave him a glance. He didn't smile or make a crack, he just gave Catell a cold stare.

They shuffled around the room, moving chairs and hanging up their hats.

"One of you gimme a hand," the sheriff said, and left the room with one of the men. Catell stood in his cell, suspicious, waiting for the next trick. That's when he heard the noise.

Outside his window in the deserted space behind the jail there was a rustling and the sound of low voices. Catell moved to the window slowly and leaned his arm on the sill. The darkness outside was almost complete and a cold breeze made him shiver in his moist shirt.

There they were, beside his car. The rear door was open, one figure had crawled into the back, and the other was leaning in, straining, as if lifting a great weight. When they hauled out the rear seat, Catell grasped the bars of the window. A stiff, sharp fear tensed his body and he trembled violently. The taut skin on his swollen hand cracked, but he didn't notice. He only saw the two figures carrying the rear seat of his car and then disappearing. In a few moments the door in the front of the jail opened and the two men came in, carrying the seat between them. They had removed the lead apron and presumably left it in the car. They put the seat on the floor. The sheriff said something about the damn weight of the thing and somebody answered with a joke, but Catell hardly heard. He sank down on the cot, feeble and numb with lost hope. How did they know? How had they found the place so fast?

Head down, hands limp between his knees, he sat not caring, not hearing the voices. Only a while later did he start to wonder what they were waiting for. In the other room the men were sitting around a flat box, talking in low voices, playing cards. Some sat on chairs, others on a bench, and the sheriff on Catell's car seat.

"Put up or shut up," said one of the players.

The sheriff was chewing on a cigar. He threw his cards down and said, "Damn you, Shivers, I'm out."

Catell threw his head back and started to laugh. He laughed loud, hard, and with a shrill fury. When he looked again the sheriff was standing by the iron door, fumbling with the lock.

"Come out, you bastard." He flung the door open.

"Tell 'im, Harry. Tell 'im you don't always lose." The men laughed. They were looking toward the cell.

Catell got off his cot and walked to the open door with an arrogant swing, grinning. When the two men were face to face, the sheriff took one step backward. He crouched.

"All right, city feller, smile good. There won't be nothin' to smile at when I get through with you."

His voice was low and hoarse, but Catell kept grinning. He stood easily, never taking his eyes off the sheriff's face. Then he took one step closer to the sheriff. The sheriff hesitated a moment, shot a quick glance at the card players behind him, but he saw they weren't looking. The sheriff straightened up, his voice loud now.

"Try something, hog face. Go ahead!"

Catell just stood still, fixing the raging man with his eyes.

"Go ahead, you bastard. Hit me!" The sheriff's voice was cracking. His head was thrust out, the cords of his neck twitching, and slobber came through the hole in his teeth. Catell could feel the man's breath.

"Hit me!"

One of the players turned around.

"Harry, for chrissakes, pipe down."

"Come on, you yellow, no-good sonofabitch, hit me!"

"Harry, boy, stop that yelling." They kept on with the cards.

Catell didn't move a muscle. He stood still, a slight smile on his face, and his voice was even.

"Did you want something, Sheriff?"

"Hit me!" The sheriff's voice was a screech.

"Do we deal you in this time, Harry?" One man was shuffling the cards; another was lighting his cigar; some were arguing about the game. Catell stepped back into his cell and pulled the door shut. Then he sat down on his cot and looked at the ceiling.

"You're yellow, you bastard. You lousy, stinking sonofabitch of a bastard!" The sheriff was shaking the bars of the cell, his face red, his voice a harsh, rasping scream. "You no-good, chicken-livered bastard, you're yellow!" he screamed.

One of the men came up and took the sheriff by the arm. "Stop that yellin', Harry. We're trying to get a game started."

"Lemme at that bastard! I'll kill 'im, I tell ya, I'll kill 'im!"

"Now shut your mouth, damnit. Sit down over here and shut up. Else we take the game to Charlie's."

"Take your lousy game to hell for all I care. Leggo my arm. You're interfering with the law."

"Harry, for chrissakes—"

The men had stopped their playing and were standing around, undecided.

"Nobody interferes with the law around here, unner-stand? Nobody! I'm gonna teach that filthy jailbird a lesson he ain't gonna forget any too soon. And you guys, stick around if you wanna have some fun. Stick around and I'll show ya how to enforce the law around here."

But they weren't listening to his raving. One by one they took their hats and walked out of the door.

"We'll be at Charlie's if you want in," said the last one. "See ya, Harry."

The sheriff stood in the empty room. Panting, cursing under his breath, he kicked the door shut and walked around the empty chairs and boxes a few times. Then he sat down on the car seat. The sheriff's hunched figure moved only with his breathing, and there was an expectant glint in Catell's eyes as he watched him.

For a while nothing happened. In the silence the thudding of a moth against the bare light bulb made a noise like a wet rag. With an irritated motion the sheriff tore his hat off and flung it at the light. He missed. Catell snickered in his dark cell. The sheriff jumped around as if stung. He got up from the seat slowly and walked to a part of the room that Catell couldn't see. When he came back, he carried a six-shooter and a long stick.

Standing by the cell, he peered into the darkness. "City feller, did you say something?"

Catell snickered again. When the sheriff came toward him, kicking the cell door aside with his foot, Catell knew this was the pay-off. He also knew that the man at the door was a coward, dangerous because he was afraid, but weak because he was unsure.

"You want something, Sheriff?"

"Come over here with your hands up!"

Catell did.

"Now walk thataway, down the hall. Stop."

This suited Catell fine. They were alone and they could not be seen from the outside.

"And now, jailbird, turn around."

Catell turned, watching the sheriff, who stood in a crouch. Catell noticed that the gun hung loosely, but the hand that held the stick was tense, with knuckles white. The sheriff wasn't thinking of doing any killing; he was going to have some sport. Then later, maybe, if he could make it look like an escape…

"Just so we understand each other, jailbird, I'm about to make you over."

"Don't call me jailbird."

"What!" The sheriff leaned forward, startled by Catell's matter-of-fact tone. His face reddened and he sucked in his breath. "Are you telling me what to do? You talking back to me, jailbird?"

Catell didn't answer. He just watched the man, who was starting to tremble with rage.

"Say something, jailbird! Open that filthy mouth once more!" The sheriff prodded his stick at Catell.

At that instant Catell whipped out his hand and yanked at the stick. The sheriff, stiff with hate and fear, stumbled forward and caught Catell's foot under his jaw. The gun clattered against the wall. Catell reached for the man's ears and jerked hard, and both men spun to the floor. Before the sheriff could start to struggle, Catell's weight jammed the wind out of his chest and two thumbs dug painfully into his Adam's apple.

"Now I'm going to do the talking, Harry, and listen

close. You called me a jailbird. Well, you're right. I can bust out of better jails than yours, but you aren't getting a thing on me that you can prove. So I'm sticking around a short while longer, but you better learn how to behave yourself. I want you to lay off, hear? I want you to lay off or else you're going to be the one that gets hurt. Because one day after I'm out of here, you're going to get a visit the likes of which you've never seen, except maybe in the movies. I got connections, Harry boy. I won't even come back here myself to make a cripple out of you for life. I know plenty of eager young boys who'd break your legs on my say-so, or dig your eyes out for a sawbuck. So lay off me, Harry boy, or haven't I made myself clear?"

Catell gave a sudden sharp squeeze to the sheriff's neck. Then he jumped up.

"Did I make myself clear?"

The sheriff, face blue, gasping for air, got up on one arm.

"Did I make myself clear?"

Catell kicked his foot at the man's arm, digging his toe painfully into a muscle.

"What's your answer, Harry?"

With an effort that made the tears shoot into his eyes, the sheriff gagged out a word: "Yes."

"That's fine, Harry. Now, I'm going back to my cell. I'm expecting a good night's sleep, so keep your voice down and step lightly. But lightly, Harry boy."

Then Catell walked to the toilet. He washed his hands, dried them, and threw the towel on the floor. The nail on which the towel had been hanging was big and loose. Catell pulled it out and stuck it in his pocket. Then he went to his cell, clanked the door shut, and stretched out on his cot.

After a little while the sheriff came by. There still was a heavy wheezing in his throat and he didn't look right or left. He sat down heavily on Catell's car seat, arms folded, looking like a man in deep thought. When the front door opened, he hardly turned his head.

"Say, Harry, you comin' over to the game? We're movin' to Rodney's place."

"Beat it."

The man hesitated, then put his hand on the doorknob.

"Just thought I'd let you know. Rodney's place, case you change your mind." He went out.

In the middle of the night Catell woke from the throbbing in his hand. Sitting up, he saw that the light in the room up front was still burning. The sheriff, head sunk on his chest, sat asleep on the car seat. Catell saw it and laughed to himself.

The next morning Catell woke early, uncomfortable and stiff. The sheriff was still asleep on the seat, and Catell laughed again.

During the next week nobody moved the car seat. It stood in the middle of the room, and ranchers dropped around and sat in the seat, and the sheriff sat there. The sheriff used the seat every day, sitting around brooding or looking out the door.

Catell was left alone. He busied himself with the nail he had taken from the toilet, bending it and flattening one end as best he could. Nobody paid much attention to the prisoner, least of all the sheriff, who acted dull and sickish. The day he threw up the first time, Catell finished with his nail. That same evening the sheriff had a sharp headache and bad cramps in his stomach. Catell laughed.

The next morning when the sheriff came to the jailhouse feeling weak and nervous he found Catell's cell empty and a crooked nail on the floor by the door. He saw that the car seat had been moved. Some stuffing was strewn around the floor and there was a big, empty hole in the seat.

Chapter Eight

By the time Catell hit Los Angeles he was broke. He got out of the Greyhound at the Sixth Street station, wearing a wrinkled suit, a dirty shirt, and a two-day growth of beard. He had lost his tan and a lot of weight. Catell didn't look so good.

The station was full of bums and drifters trying to keep out of the cold night air. Catell got lost in the crowd easily. Once he was sure that nobody was looking for him, he went outside and turned toward Main. With his hands in his pocket he jingled some coins, counting them for the thousandth time. Ninety-eight cents. About eighty miles out of Los Angeles he had buried his gold where nobody would look for it. Catell thought about his gold, $20,160 worth. He jingled his coins again. He was broke.

Main Street was twice as windy as Sixth and Catell turned up the collar of his suit. When he came to a bar he went in. The narrow room was full of smoke, sour and thick. But it was warm. At the far end of the counter where they sold hamburgers and coffee, Catell sat down. The grill made a greasy warmth. Catell ordered coffee.

On one side of him a shrill-looking whore was eating a doughnut that left sugar grains sticking to her lipstick. On the other side two bums were making a coffee royal with gin. Behind him people were pushing by to go to the john or to get out of the draft from the door. Catell felt a slight pressure at his pocket. His hand reached back fast; his fingers closed around a wrist. An embarrassed face peered at him when Catell turned.

"Pardon me, mister. A natural mistake."

"Your last, dippy." Catell grabbed for the small man's shirt front.

"Tony!"

"For chrissakes, if it isn't the Turtle!"

"Well, Tony!"

"Not so loud, not so loud."

They looked at each other, grinning, not knowing exactly what to do next.

"How about my wrist, Anthony feller? How about letting me recuperate my wrist?"

Catell let go and grinned. "You're losing your touch, Turtle. You're not doing so good."

"You may have a message there, Anthony. Indeed, indeed." And then in a serious tone: "Just rusty, Anthony. I'm in semi-retirement, you know."

Catell grinned at the Turtle and looked him up and down. The small man had a tight suit on, pepper and salt, but it was a good one. His pointed shoes looked scuffed, but they were expensive. As always, the Turtle's shirt was too large at the neck. Catell didn't remember the time when the Turtle's skinny neck had had a collar to fit it. But that wasn't the only reason for his name. He had a face like a turtle's: a nose and forehead shaped in a humpy curve, a thin long mouth with a chin that made a flat angle, and round eyes without lashes. The Turtle had a way of looking dreamy or astonished or dumb, and any one of these expressions was an asset in his trade.

"Semi-retirement, huh? That why you're picking on a bum like me?"

"Now, Anthony. I was just practicing. Just practicing, you understand. Coming out of winter retirement, so to speak."

"How about retiring your hand out of my pocket?"

The Turtle gave him his dumb expression, then the astonished one. He pulled his hand out of Catell's pocket and looked at it. There was ninety-eight cents in it.

"You ain't retiring, I notice."

"Just a little short this minute."

"Don't kid your old friend, Tony. You look strapped."

"Nothing to worry about. I got a deal on."

"Like eight years ago?"

"No, not like eight years ago. Never again."

"O.K., O.K., friend. I was just making merry."

"So sit down, Turtle, talk to me."

But the Turtle didn't sit.

"What time is it?"

"Eleven."

"Eleven. Recline here for a minute, Anthony. Don't move I'll be back in a shiver, so don't move. Promise."

"O.K., I'll be here."

The Turtle squeezed through the crowd and went out.

"I couldn't help hearin' you, friend," said the whore one seat down. "You sure all you got is ninety-eight cents?" She smiled, licking the sugar from her lips.

"What's it to you?"

"Just warmhearted interest. If you're broke, I thought you may be needing a flop. If you're not," and she cocked a hip, "I got another idea."

"Save it."

Catell turned his back to the woman. He could feel her looking at him and he got uncomfortable. When he turned around she caught his eye and winked.

"Cut out the kid stuff. I'm not interested."

"I wasn't trying to give you any kid stuff."

"Save it!"

"I've been!"

"Well, I don't want it."

Catell started to look for a cigarette, but before he could shake one from the pack the whore pulled one out of her purse and handed it to him. When she leaned over the V of her blouse opened up and Catell got a good look.

"Thanks."

"Don't thank me for that, baby. I got something better to offer."

"I ain't buying."

But the woman didn't give up. She swiveled on the stool and swung her leg slowly against Catell.

"Who's talkin' of buying, baby?"

Catell got impatient, but before he had opened his mouth a voice said:

"Is this lady annoying you?"

They both turned and saw the Turtle. He was wearing the dumb expression. Then he said, "Blow, lady."

"Now, listen here, runt—"

"Lady, blow. No lovers' quarrels, puleeze."

"Tell this creep to go away," she said to Catell.

The Turtle put a hand on her shoulder and spoke in a confidential tone. "Sweet, you're making too many mistakes. My friend and me are a couple of fairies, and very much in love. We're gettin' wedded tonight and no bridesmaids. So, puleeze, lady, drag outa here."

The whore gasped at the Turtle and then looked at Catell. She made an offensive sound, got up, and strutted away.

The Turtle sat down next to Catell and waved to the short-order man. "Vegetable soup, two scrambled with ham, side of fries, apple pie a la mode, glass of milk, coffee. For my friend here. For me, a spot of tea."

"Now, listen, Turtle—"

"Shut up. You're broke, I ain't."

"Turtle, not the milk."

"Shut it, Anthony. Milk's good, and you look like hell."

"You don't kid me, Turtle. You don't look so hot yourself."

The Turtle didn't answer. He pulled bills out of various pockets and folded them together. Then he stuck the money away.

"You were speaking to me, Anthony?"

"Where'd that come from, all of a sudden?"

"Where else?"

"You were only gone about fifteen minutes."

"A master does not need time, only opportunity."

"Opportunity on Main Street, L.A. Don't tell me!"

"I did the movie crowd on Broadway. Deceived by the balmy breezes of our daytime weather, few citizens were wearing coats tonight. A true blessing to the likes of me and the likes of your empty stomach. Now stop crapping and eat."

Catell ate and they didn't talk for a while. The Turtle sipped his tea, trying to look elegant with one finger sticking out. He was very proud of his delicate hands, but when he sipped the tea, he made a loud, slurpy sound with his mouth. When Catell was on his coffee, he lit a cigarette and leaned his elbows on the counter.

"Well, Turtle, say something."

"I can tell you feel better. You say something."

"What?"

"What's the big deal you got on?"

"The big deal. I need a little help, Turtle. You want in?"

"If it's within my interests, count me in."

"Is money?"

"Anthony, count me in."

"Like I said, Turtle, I need some assist. The deal is all done with, except I got to unload the swag here in town and I don't know my way around."

"Nothing's easier, Tony. Just name the name and I find. By the way, anybody looking for you?"

"Yeah, the Feds."

"Oi! They know you're here?"

"That's one of the things you gotta find out for me."

"Will do. What are they after?"

"Big-time stuff, Turtle."

"A lot of cash in it, huh?"

"Not really. Not that much, but it's big-time, Turtle, and I pulled it off neat. No hitch so far."

"Dope?"

"Naw. Gold."

"You mean—you mean a solid, pure block of it? Nothing but gold?

"Uh-huh."

Turtle closed his eyes and hummed through his lips, low and long. "Now, that kind of merchandise, Anthony, you can sell *anywhere.*"

"No, that's just it. It turns out the stuff is radioactive or something. Some kind of rays that get to you, because it was accidentally exposed to one of those atom piles. It makes you sick."

"That sick I'd like to be."

"Anyway, I don't know the details. All I know is there may be a contact for the stuff in this town."

"Who?"

"Smith. S. S. Smith, I think."

"Oi! Contact, he says. Smith ain't no contact, Tony boy. Smith is it!"

"All right, fine. Where is he?"

"Where is he? Where is he, he says." Turtle clapped his hands around his throat. "Now listen, Tony. I want you to understand something. Nobody goes and sees Smith. Smith sends for the people he wants to see, and that ain't many."

"All right, stop with the courtesies. You sound like the Chamber of Commerce. Where is Smith?"

"Tony, to tell the truth, I ain't sure. Who told ya, anyway?"

"Some guy back in Detroit. He was bragging about his big-shot contacts and out slipped the name. So from then on I didn't need the guy back in Detroit, see?"

"Yeah, I see. You ever deal with the syndicate before, Tony?"

"No. Why?"

"I'm trying to tell ya. They are big, complicated, like a corporation. Like a government. You don't just walk in, you see. They got red tape to go through."

"Just how big is this Smith?"

"Locally, very big."

"The biggest?"

"No—not for sure, anyway."

"All right, Turtle, when do I find this big shot?"

"Lemme find out for sure, Tony, willya? Lemme listen around, get everything set up, and then we make our pitch."

"Nuts to that. I gotta get this thing over with. Ninety-eight cents isn't even life-size these days."

"I'll stake ya, Tony. You gotta play the angles a little in this town before you get anyplace. Like for instance, your suit looks like hell. You need new shoes."

"You said you'd stake me."

"Sure, sure, but give it time."

"I'm going to find that guy tomorrow, Turtle, with you or without you."

"All right, I give up. There's a machine shop on Victory Boulevard in Burbank. The Quentin Machine Company. Try there. Smith's got an office in the back there. Maybe you're in luck. Does he know you're coming?"

"Might be. I don't know."

"Whaddaya mean ya don't know?"

"That guy in Detroit. He might or he might not have passed the word. I don't know."

"Anthony, you're looking more stupid to me by the minute. Either—"

"Can it. I'm going tomorrow. What I need from you is a few bucks to get a shirt and a press job. Also, keep your ears open about those Feds. Also, I want to know everything you can get ahold of about my deal with Smith. If I can make a deal with Smith tomorrow, I want to know how they feel about it, who's in on it, et cetera. The works, hear?"

"I hear."

"Can you do it?"

"Anthony, you are looking at the original underground kid. I get to know everything."

"You sound better already. From here on in, Turtle, you and me hit the big time. With this job out of the way, I got a career ahead of me. Shake?"

"Shake. And now, mine Anthony, how about the last cup of mud and we blow?"

"Let's just blow. I gotta find a flop yet."

"Flop? Anthony! Cart that thought outen your vocabulary. It so happens I got an extra corner in my room, and you're staying with me. On second thought, you look too tacky for the likes of my accommodations. First I take you to a Turkish bath. Whilst you melt your tackiness with steam and soap, I get your suit done over and fetch a new shirt. And underwear?"

"Yeah. Underwear. And socks."

"And socks. Only then, Anthony, will we be off to my chamber and a good night's rest. Ready?"

"Let's go."

They left the bar and walked a few blocks to the Turkish bath. As they went up the stairs, the flashy whore from the bar was coming down. She stopped swinging her hips and leaned against the wall to let them pass. The Turtle stopped next to her and chucked the woman under the chin.

"You work here too, honey?"

She made that nasty sound with her lips again.

"Whyn't you go blow?" she said.

"Precisely," and with a busy look on his face the Turtle ran up the stairs after Catell.

In the small lobby Catell took the Turtle aside. "What the hell is this place, coeducational?"

"Whassa matter, Anthony, you prejudiced or something?"

"I want a steam bath and a wash is all."

"If that's what you pay for, that's all you get. Now stop worrying about the opposition sex and let's have those raggedy garnishments you're wearing."

A little later the Turtle left with Catell's suit and shoes. Catell took a steam bath, showered and shaved, and after his massage he went to the locker room. An attendant brought him his pressed suit, clean socks, underwear, and a new shirt. His shoes were polished.

"Your friend left 'em, with a note."

Catell read the note: "Dear Anthony. Got tired of waiting. When done come to my place," and then there was an address. It was signed, "T."

Catell got dressed and combed his hair. He was feeling good. In the mirror he noticed that his shirt collar was a little big. Either he had lost more weight than he'd realized or the Turtle was constitutionally incapable of buying a shirt that would fit anyone.

Outside, Catell walked fast to keep from shivering. After a few blocks he came to the address on the Turtle's note and walked in. It was a narrow apartment house converted into a hotel, gloomy and crowded-looking. But it was warm inside. Catell went past the clerk, past a pimply bellhop who was sleeping in a swivel chair, and walked up to the second floor. He stopped before the door with the number 206. Then he heard the movement inside. There was a slight rustle and a low voice. Two voices. The mumbling stopped. Catell stood frozen in the still corridor, a curse twisting his face. What had gone wrong?

He turned carefully and started to walk back to the stairwell when a door at the end of the dim corridor creaked. He flattened himself against the wall, his blood throbbing under his skull. The door clicked shut and a figure came toward the stairwell. It was a man. He looked like a bum, but so what? Then the man turned down the stairs, never looking in Catell's direction. Licking his dry lips, Catell started to move when the voice behind 206 started to mumble again. Then there was a cackling laugh —the Turtle's laugh. Catell pushed open the door and looked in. There was no light in the room, just the red reflection from a gas heater that stood near one wall. The light showed the bare legs of a woman who was shaking a skirt down over her head, and it showed the droopy pajamas of a short man. When Catell clicked the door shut, the Turtle turned around, looking surprised.

"Why, Tony, we thought you'd never come. Didn't we, sweetness?"

The woman had the skirt down now and pulled the zipper over her hip. She was still naked from the waist up, her big breasts making a billowing shadow on the wall. She turned and Catell recognized the whore from the bar.

"For chrissakes, you again?"

"It's destiny," said the Turtle. "I always say, don't try to buck destiny. What do you say, Millie?"

"I say, speaking of a buck—" and she planted her hands on her hips and looked hard at the Turtle.

After the Turtle had given her a bill she picked up her brassiere and slipped the straps over her shoulders. She did it slowly, looking at Catell with a mean look on her face. Catell didn't think she looked so bad at all, and he leaned back in his chair. He fumbled for a cigarette, looking at the woman in the red light from the heater. She pulled the cups of the brassiere around her breasts and arched her back to hook the clasp. Catell noticed how the big shadow on the wall had changed shape. Then he looked back at her.

"One more look and you pay," she said to Catell.

He grinned.

"Throw me my blouse, Daisy," she said.

Catell threw her the thin blouse. She put it on and Catell watched how it buttoned tight across the front.

"Now the shoes. Under your chair, Mary."

"You don't need 'em," Catell said.

"The shoes, Mary. I'm a respectable woman. I wear shoes."

"The hell with the shoes. You look more sexy with your feet naked."

"Come on, faggot, the shoes," and she stamped her foot.

"Do that again, baby. It makes you wiggle so nice." Catell grinned at her. She came at him with mouth curled back over her teeth and her loose hair flying. When she reached out to claw at him, Catell caught her wrists and pinned her arms to her sides. Trying to wrench free, she popped a button and the blouse fell open.

"I get more cooperation from that button than I get from you," he said.

"I told ya I'm a respectable woman," she hissed, kicking at him.

The Turtle had picked up his bathrobe and was just opening the door to go out.

"Leave some dough on the table. Millie's going to earn it." Catell leaned over to reach her mouth and she bit him. He jerked back and laughed. "Millie's gonna make whoopee with a fruitcake, ha, Millie?"

The door shut behind the Turtle and Catell reached for the woman's straps. She stepped back fast, knocking his hands out of the way and lashing at his face. Her nails cut a fine line of blood down his cheek and her other hand caught him flat on the nose. Catell stumbled back, cursing, and fell over the chair. When he looked up she was standing near the rim of the red reflection. Her skirt was a heap on the floor, and the light made dim patterns on her bare legs and belly. Then the blouse fell off, and the brassiere. When the woman was naked she came at him again, but she didn't try to scratch this time.

Chapter Nine

Catell left for Burbank at nine in the morning. For the next five hours he shuffled back and forth in one bus after another, missing stops, rooting around for a connection, letting a bus go by to catch a bite at a street stand. By the middle of the day the hot sun had brewed up a smog that burned in Catell's eyes and made the inside of his nose feel like shoe leather. When he got out on Victory and found the Quentin Machine Company, he was grimy with sweat and sore.

Inside the shop it felt hotter than outside. A couple of big fans swished the oily air around so that the draft made you feel prickly with dirt.

"Yes, sir, you lookin' for somethin'?"

A thin man in clean, starched suntans came up to Catell and stopped in front of him.

"I'm looking for Smith," Catell said.

The thin guy took his rimless glasses off, put them back on again, and patted himself on his bald head. Catell noticed how the man looked dry all over. Why didn't that bastard sweat like everybody else?

"We got two Smiths here. Kind of a common name, I guess. Which Smith you innerested in?"

"S. Smith."

"Sherman!" the man yelled. "Come here once."

A man who had been working on a drill press came down the aisle between the machines and looked at Catell.

"Yeah?"

"You S. Smith?" Catell asked.

"Yeah. Who are you? Do I know you?"

"I just came in from Detroit. Friend of Paar's."

"Paar? You got the wrong guy, feller. I don't know no Paar."

"Sorry, my mistake," Catell said. "Perhaps the other Smith is the one I want." He turned back to the man in suntans.

"Might be, except that he ain't here today. Hurt his hand on the shaper. Hot chips, ya know, burned a hole right in his arm. You go back, Sherman. Guess you're the wrong guy."

Catell watched the machinist walk back to his drill press. That wasn't the Smith he wanted, and his Smith hadn't got hurt working on a shaper, either.

"There's another Smith here," Catell said. "He doesn't work on a machine. He's got an office here and I want to see him."

"Well, now, I'm the foreman here and there's no other Smith works here. Who're you, anyway?"

"Where's the office?"

"I guess you didn't hear me, mister. What's your name and business?"

Catell gave the foreman a bland look. "I guess you didn't hear me, either. Where's the office?"

"Mister, I don't need to tell you anything, but just to get rid of you, I got my desk right over yonder." He pointed to a windowless corner with a desk and files separated from the rest of the shop by some badly tacked beaverboard.

"There's another office. Where is it?" Catell took a step.

The thin guy in suntans stuck his arm out and held

Catell by the lapels. "No further, mister." He pulled Catell close.

The two men stared at each other, almost nose to nose.

"Tell me, foreman, how come you don't sweat?"

The man didn't answer.

"I said, how come you don't sweat?" Catell jabbed two fingers into the man's stomach.

The foreman let go of Catell's lapels. "You lookin' for trouble, mister, you got it." Wheezing in his throat, he swung at Catell with a flabby roundhouse. Catell just stepped back, right into the arms of two machinists. They twisted Catell's arms in opposite directions and, with his feet hardly touching the ground, walked him to the rear of the shop.

There was another door there. Through the tool crib and past a noisy pump motor there was another office. The foreman opened the door, the two machinists gave a light push, and Catell stumbled into the room. The foreman kicked the door shut and Catell couldn't hear the pump motor any more. He suddenly felt pleasantly cool.

Aside from the soundproofing and the air conditioning, there was nothing special about the room. White composition walls, a leatherette couch, a small desk with three phones, no windows. The light came from fluorescent fixtures in the ceiling.

"Don't try anything, mister. You and I ain't alone here."

"I figured we weren't," Catell said. He got off the floor and watched the foreman go through another door. Catell sat down on the couch. He couldn't hear a sound except for the faint humming of the air conditioning. Then the foreman came back. Without bothering to look at Catell he walked past and out through the soundproofed door. A while later the inner door opened again.

The man was well built and well tailored. He had glossy hair and his mouth was very red. If this was a syndicate man, Catell figured him for one of those smart young kids who came up fast because he knew how to take orders without questions, and how to follow through without scruples.

Tailor-made stopped opposite Catell and gave him a dead look.

"What's your name?"

"What's yours?"

For a second the dead look came alive and Catell thought the guy was going to jump him, but then he relaxed and sat on the edge of the desk.

"You got this wrong, Blue Lips," he said. "I don't answer, I ask. And you, Blue Lips, you answer what I ask. Now, what's your name?"

"If you're Smith, I'll talk. If not, I don't talk."

"I'm Smith, Blue Lips. Mr. Smith, that is."

"O.K. My name's Catell. Tony Catell. I got your name from a friend of mine in Detroit. Paar's his name. If you got the time, I'd like to talk to you about something."

"I got the time, Blue Lips. Talk."

Catell didn't like the way things were going, and the tailor-made punk was getting under his skin. What made Catell really hot was the fact that he'd been had. This punk wasn't S. S. Smith any more than the foreman had been a big shot. No big shot talked tough like a punk.

"Call me that name once more and the next time you look in the shaving mirror you won't recognize the face you see. Now where's Smith?"

Catell noticed that the guy didn't move after the speech. He saw him go stiff and his chin started to quiver, as if he wanted to cry. He didn't cry, though. The next thing Catell saw was the business end of a banker's special, and Tailor-made was holding it. He was holding it very steady.

"What name you talking about, Blue Lips?" His voice sounded very gentle.

Catell looked at the steady gun and then there was the sound of shoes creaking. The gun came closer. It was very still in the room, just the slow creak of the new shoes. Catell's shirt felt wet and clammy on his back, and he started to rise.

"Go ahead, Blue Lips. You can get up if you want." That voice was as smooth as silk.

Then it was very quiet again. The shoes had stopped creaking, the gun was very close. Suddenly there was a sharp, nasty sound, loud like a splintering tree. The gun was cocked now. Cold with sweat, Catell looked up at the man's face. The lidded eyes looked soft, the mouth was lax and very red, and nothing moved but the chin, still quivering. Then Catell saw the man's neck. It was a smooth neck, and with a weird fascination Catell could see how the neck was swelling. Slowly it started to bulge over the starched collar and a thick vein grew under the skin, like a glistening worm.

Then the mouth moved and the soft voice said, "Now, Blue Lips?"

"Now what, gentlemen?"

They both jumped. A portly man stood by the inner door, his short arms folded across his front, and he was smiling around a cigar.

There was no emotion in the way the gunman moved. He stepped back slowly, turned his head toward the open door, and slipped the gun very smoothly under his tailor-made jacket.

"Mr. Smith," he said. "I didn't know you were there."

"I know," Mr. Smith said. "I was just watching."

Catell wasn't taking the whole thing so lightly. When the gun had disappeared he had suddenly felt very weak. He sank back on the couch, wiping the sweat from his face. He noticed that his hands were shaking when he dropped them back to his lap. There was a fine sharp pain running up his arm from his left hand. There, on the back of it, he saw the reddish skin of the healed wound where the sheriff had sapped him. Only the skin wasn't all healed. It had cracked again and a little dark blood was running out.

"Did you hurt Mr.—ah, Mr.—?" Smith looked concerned.

"I didn't touch him. His name's Catell."

"Is this true, Mr. Catell?"

"You Smith?" Catell was back on his feet, but his voice had a sudden crack in it.

"*Mr.* Smith," said the punk. He stepped up to Catell and grabbed him by the lapels. "The name to you is *Mr.* Smith," and he jerked the lapels hard. Catell didn't try to resist. His head had started to spin and he felt like a rag. Then his strength came back as suddenly as it had gone, but now Smith had come up close.

"You may stop that," he said to the gunman, and there was a hint of coldness in his voice. "And you, sir, I'm sure you will overlook our hot-blooded friend. Would you care to introduce yourself properly now?"

Catell shook his jacket back into shape and ran his fingers through his hair.

"Sure. As your friend said, my name's Catell. Tony Catell. A friend of mine in Detroit—"

"Paar," said Smith. "Yes, I've heard of you. And you wanted to speak to me?"

"If you got the time."

"Come in, come in. There's been too much ceremony already, so let's sit down and get to it." He laughed with a short, hiccuppy gurgle.

The inner office was larger than the anteroom, but it looked much smaller, full with a large desk, couch, chairs, files, and telephones.

Smith sat down behind the desk and Catell settled himself into an easy chair. Tailor-made put his hand on the back of the chair, the knuckles touching Catell's shoulder.

Smith looked at Catell with a winning smile on his round face, and Catell looked back at Smith, trying to get his bearings. For a while nobody said anything.

"Well, Catell, let me help you along. I understand from your good friend Paar that you have something to sell. Now you, of course, know nothing about me, except that I'm a friend of Paar's, that I do business on the West Coast, and that I might be able to help you. Now then, what's your story?"

"How about Monkey Boy here? How about him getting the hell outa here?"

"Oh, well now," said Smith, and he made benign sounds.

Catell turned around in his seat, looking up at the gunman. They stared at each other without moving.

Smith said, "You were saying, Catell?"

"I wasn't saying anything. And I'm not saying anything, Smith, unless Monkey Boy gets out."

A knuckle dug into Catell's shoulder from behind and the gentle voice said, "It's *Mr.* Smith, Blue Lips."

Catell jumped up, kicking the chair backward. It didn't move much, but the gunman stumbled. Half crouched, he was reaching into his jacket when Catell gave the chair another kick. The back of the chair slapped the gunman's knees, making him buckle again. With the edge of his hand Catell knifed down on the man's neck, jamming his face down against the top of the chair. But when the man rolled over, half on the floor now, the gun was in his hand and coming up fast.

"Enough!" Smith's voice was sharp.

Catell saw that the gun stopped moving instantly and then disappeared again under the jacket.

"In fact, I think you'd better leave. I won't need you now. I feel Mr. Catell and I will get along quite nicely. I can reach you at the club?"

"Sure, Mr. Smith." The gunman got off the floor. His face was soft and calm. Without looking at Catell he turned and went out. Catell noticed he was carrying his head at a slight angle.

"I'm sorry you had this little brush," Smith said. "Topper is a very fine young man. A little too exacting sometimes, but perhaps for that reason particularly valuable to me."

There was a noticeable undertone in Smith's words, the kind of tone that Catell would ordinarily resent. But he hadn't caught it. He'd caught only the name Topper, and there was a thin twitch in Catell's left cheek. He ran a hand over his face and sat down again.

"Do you know what I'm selling, Smith?"

"No, I have no idea. I am interested, though, because of Paar's—ah—recommendation. He doesn't phone me too often, but he did feel obliged to tell me about you. What are you selling, Catell?"

"Gold."

Smith didn't answer right away. He just sat with his hands folded, smiling at Catell.

"Did you say gold? Plain gold?"

"Yeah, plain gold."

There was another silence while Smith pulled his lower lip and looked at Catell with that smile.

"Let's understand each other, Catell," he said finally. "What you have isn't plain gold. It's radioactive gold."

Catell didn't back down under the voice. He leaned forward in his chair and looked at Smith with a plain, hostile stare. "All I know for sure is I got gold. Maybe it's radioactive, maybe it isn't. When it's radioactive, the stuff makes you sick, doesn't it? Well, I'm not sick. I've had it with me for a while now and I'm O.K."

"You still have the gold then?"

"I've got it."

"Have you seen it lately?"

"I've got it and I want to sell it."

Smith swiveled his chair to face in the opposite direction. With head back, he sat like that for several minutes, thinking. There were a lot of things that Smith knew about. He knew about business, about organizing men, about demand and supply, he even knew about scientific things. When he'd organized his territory for prostitution, he'd got together information on incidence of venereal disease, on percentages of income groups patronizing whorehouses. When he'd heard about Catell's heist, he'd studied the properties of radioactive substances, gold in particular. What he was not sure about was whether the gold had actually been made radioactive. Scientists and FBI men were the worst sources of information.

"So you say you have this gold, eh, Catell?"

"Look, Smith, like you said, let's understand each other. Either you want it or you don't. Say no, and I leave. Say yes, and we talk terms."

For just a moment Smith didn't move at all. Then he

leaned forward on the desk and chuckled with a wet sound. "Catell, I like that. Of course I believe you. Not only because you are that kind of man, but also because, after all, there's no percentage in your lying to me. In fact— But let it go. So you want to sell your gold. I want to buy it. How much have you and how much do you want?"

"I got thirty-six pounds—regular pounds like in weighing machines, not troy pounds. At thirty-five dollars a troy ounce, that comes to twenty thousand, one hundred and sixty dollars. On the market, I understand, it's worth more. About twenty-eight thousand. I'll give it to you for twenty even. Well?"

"Mr. Catell, I'd like to help you, but that's more than I can pay."

"Whaddaya mean, more than you can pay? You broke or something?"

Smith hiccupped and gurgled his laugh for a while and then stopped abruptly.

"No, Catell, it's not that I'm broke. I'm experienced, though, and while I've never handled this large a piece of gold, I predict it's not going to be easy to move. Please don't interrupt. You want to tell me that lump gold is one of the easiest things to move. Perhaps. But are you forgetting that this stuff may have radioactive properties? And even if it doesn't, it still has that reputation. All in all, Catell, the circumstances of the entire deal you pulled tend to limit the number of potential customers quite radically. And that, you know, means more work for me, more risk, and therefore less money for you."

"How much less?"

"Twelve thousand dollars."

Catell jumped out of his chair and leaned over Smith's

desk. "Smith," he said, "why don't you go drop dead?"
Then he straightened up and started to turn.

"Wait a minute. Sit down, Catell. Now, look. The least
you should get out of this is some good advice. How long
have you been out of stir?"

"Two months."

"And you act like it. I can see your point of view. Here
you get out, pull a brilliant piece of work, and naturally
expect your recognition. Well, times have been changing.
First of all, your lone-wolf type of operation doesn't
mean so much anymore. We work by organization these
days. Secondly, things have got tight. In money and
everything else. Did you know Slater, biggest fence operation in the Frisco area? Well, he's locked away. Or Jensen
in New Orleans, imports and exports, if you know what I
mean? He got life. And so it goes. Let me advise you,
Catell, count your friends, take your pay, and learn to
play ball."

"I know one thing, Smith: You're offering me less than
that crook Paar. How do you account for that?"

"Catell, please." Smith sounded pained. "Personally,
I like you. In fact, knowing your quality of work, I respect
you. Well, look, Catell. What do you say to fifteen thousand? I'm honestly trying to help you. What do you say?"

"No."

"No? Catell, you've got to wake up. There's nothing
else that anybody can do for you. You're lucky you came
to me, because even though you may not know it, I'm
taking a personal interest in you. And do you want to
know why? Because, like I said, I admire your work. I
have good men in my organization, believe me, but they
aren't artists. In fact, artists are getting few and far
between. So, call it sentimental if you want, I'd like to do

you a good turn. However, you're asking too much, Catell, way too much."

Catell had been sucking on a cigarette, only half listening to Smith buttering him up. What did the bastard want from him?

"Listen, Catell, I just had an idea. Ah, have you ever considered working for us?"

"I've had bad moments like that, Smith, but I'm not having one now. Right now, I'm trying to talk a deal with you, nothing else."

"So am I, Catell, so am I. By the way, you're broke, aren't you?"

"I'm getting by."

"Sure. Just about. Are you getting by enough to say no to five hundred down?"

"Down for what?"

"Here's what I have in mind, Catell. You want to move your swag? Fine. You want to move it at your price? Fine again. I'll give you what you ask, twenty thousand. But as I've been trying to explain, Catell, I'll be overpaying you. So it's no more than a square deal for you to trade me something else. I'm talking about your experience, Catell. Now, shut up a minute. I don't want you to underestimate yourself, because you have something we can use. I'm not asking you to come in with us. Just hiding out, I'd call it. So here's the deal: I give you twenty thousand for the gold, and you come in on one deal we've got coming up. What's more, we'll pay you for your services, and as a friend, here's five hundred down."

Smith leaned back in his chair and looked at Catell, putting a hopeful smile on his face.

"It's no good, Smith. All I want to do is sell my swag."

Smith's smile dropped, but he didn't look disappointed. He just said, "Take it or leave it, Catell."

There was a cold silence. Catell knew that aside from a slight blow to his pride, nobody was getting hurt in this deal. If Smith was on the level. Smith just had to be on the level. Guys like him paid for services rendered and that was that. And then there was five hundred cash, more cash to come, and all this on top of finally moving the gold.

"When do I get the cash for my gold?"

"After the other deal."

The bastard!

"And what's my cut for the other deal?"

"A flat fifteen hundred. No cut out of the swag. Just a flat fifteen hundred. After all, Catell—"

"Plus five hundred now?"

"Minus, Catell. Five hundred now, a thousand after the heist, and the gold deal after that. I'm trying to be generous with you, Catell, really I am." Smith took a stack of bills out of his desk. He flapped them back and forth against one hand, smiling again.

"All right, Smith, it's a deal."

They both got to their feet. They shook hands, exchanged a silent look, and then Smith gave the bundle of notes to Catell. The wrapper was still on them, and it said "$500."

"I'm sure you won't regret this, Catell, and I'm glad to have you working for me."

"I'll do my job, Smith."

"Of course you will. Call me in two days and we'll get together for the briefing. The whole job should be duck soup for you."

"And now," said Catell, "I'll have me a go at this town. And a few clothes would be in order. By the way, what's that club you mentioned before?"

"The Pink Shell. Topper runs it for me."

"That figures."

"Now, there are some other places you probably haven't seen yet. The Hideaway, or the—"

"Pink Shell sounds fine, Smith. Where is it?"

"You go out to Malibu. Do you know the way to Santa Barbara? It's on that highway, just the other side of Malibu. A very nice place, Catell, you can have a lot of fun there— that is, if you stay friends with Topper. And I might mention, Catell, I don't like quarrels in my organization."

"Listen, Smith, I only—"

"Of course, you're just here to help me out with one little job, so all this talk is really unnecessary. But while you're here, Catell, try to keep clear of Topper, eh?"

"Sure, Smith, sure. I'm not going out there to see Topper."

For the rest of the day Catell kept thinking of the Pink Shell and what he thought he might find there.

Chapter Ten

Chief Jones watched the teletype ticking out the end of Herron's sentence: "...therefore requesting your decision for possible change in present plan."

Jones tore the sheet off the machine, looked at it again, and then stepped over to the window. The St. Louis traffic was crawling along four stories down, and Jones wondered what he would do if he had to find the person with the brown hat who was just crossing against the light, and if he could ever get anywhere with his strategies, scientific methods, trained agents, and what have you, unless of course he had an informer to steer him the right way. Perhaps that man in the brown hat who was now turning the corner by the newsstand was Catell. Or perhaps Jack Herron in Los Angeles wasn't having any success, not even a false steer, because Catell was dead someplace, dead from radiation, or starvation, or too much liquor, or too many women.

If only they knew a little more about the man. He'd been operating for years and years, he'd been caught three times, but he'd never been so successful or so menacing or so crazy that the name Anthony Catell had meant a whole lot. Catell worked fast, like an expert, and then he'd disappear. He had probably pulled twice as many jobs as he'd ever been suspected of having pulled. Not a very encouraging train of thought. Or let's say Catell is dead; then what?

The teletype started chattering again and Jones walked over. "...dead man in ravine next to abandoned car. No license plates. Initial check indicates car driven from Detroit. Age of deceased estimated 85. Cause of death, heart failure."

The thing was sent by the Indiana State Police and there was a brief reference to the FBI's request that all unusual or unexplained deaths and hospital admittances be reported.

No need to jump at that one. Jones had been getting the lowdown on the death of every bum from here to Hudson Bay and he was beginning to wonder how soon they would all die out.

The machine started to clank again but Jones barely gave it a look. "Diagnosis probable," it said, and then Jones was back at the teletype, watching the letters creep out. "Admitted 6 A.M., Winslow General Hospital, Winslow, Arizona." Then it gave the name of the patient, a sheriff in a small desert town.

He was alive. Catell was alive and Herron's first guess might still be right. Jones looked at both messages again. Michigan car abandoned in Indiana. No plates. That would be like Catell. Then he appeared to have shown up in Arizona, making the southerly swing through all the rural stretches he could find. Maybe Mexico next? They would take care of that, and Herron... Leave Herron in Los Angeles.

Chief Jones sent a message to Herron and stepped back to the window. He ran one hand over his face. For a minute there he had felt good, but it was still a wild-goose chase. He stood by the window and down at the street corner. The man in the brown hat was back. Or was it the same man? It could be one of his own agents, coming back from lunch. Didn't Malotti wear a brown hat like that?

Jones left the communications room and went back to his office. He picked up the phone and asked for Agent Kantovitz. He wasn't in. "Tell him to make another local check with his contacts on that Schumacher matter. He'll know what I mean. And Betty, do you happen to know if Malotti wears a brown hat? He does?…No, it's nothing. Forget it."

The phone jangled on Herron's desk and he looked at it for a second before answering it. Another lead, no doubt. In the movies, they always got leads coming in at the last minute. He picked up the phone.

"Hello, Herron here."

"Where else? I figured you'd be there, seeing you're answering the phone."

"Larry? What in hell you want now?"

"I got a lead for you."

"I knew it. So you got a lead for me, huh? Where's it leading to—your newspaper column?"

"Naw, listen. This may be something."

"I bet. When the FBI needs local copy boys to crack a case for 'em, then that long month of Sundays has really come."

"So this is a long month of Sundays. Oh, well, seeing you ain't interested, I think I'll talk to somebody worth while. I got a dictaphone here, for instance—"

"All right, tell me. What's this lead you got?"

"Well, you've been telling me you came here to pick up some old-time hood, and so far no luck, right?"

"Yes, I'm sorry to say."

"Well, this may or may not be anything. I was in Santa Monica last night, down in the Mexican section and had a beer with a hood friend of mine. He's pretty harmless mostly, but he's in with some of the lower-rung syndicate punks. So we were talking about this and that, me trying to get a certain thing out of him—nothing special, just something I needed for a cross check—when he ups and says, 'Larry,' he says, 'I don't know if I ought to be talkin' to you like this here,' and he clams up."

"Larry, that was very nice of you. Real nice of you to call me up and explain about this lead you got. This real hot lead! Any time you feel the urge to—"

"Will you shut up and listen? That is by no means all, you flatfoot."

"Pardon me, Larry, pardon me. So go on."

"All right, then. So I say to him, 'Hood, why the silent treatment? Why this unfriendly relationship?' So he tells me there are things brewing. 'What, what?' I say. I must have sounded eager or something, because he answers, 'Even if I knew I wouldn't tell ya.' So I switch to acting coy and disbelieving. 'You don't know nothing and this is just your way of acting big. Show-off, if you know what I mean.' This gets him. 'I know plenty,' he says. 'Just for instance,' he says, 'I know they got an import to handle a deal for them.' I say, 'An import? A torpedo? And who's gonna be pushin' daisies?' 'Naw,' he says, 'nothing like that. A jug heavy or something. All the way from out East. But I mean, all the way.' Then he goes on to brag about a dozen other things he had predicted for me, all of which was a lie, so I bought him a few more beers, but no further info.

"So that's it, Jackie. Maybe the guy you want is the same guy my hood friend was discussing, His description sort of jibes with the one you've used. Now, did I tell you something?"

Herron didn't talk for a moment, just patted his hair where it was getting thin.

"Larry," he said finally, "perhaps you do have something there. I certainly appreciate your calling. I'm going to follow this up. What's the name of this hood friend of yours?"

"Nix, Jack. Professional ethics, you know."

"Ethics? Why, you crumb, you wouldn't have a column, a single sentence of your column, if you had any ethics."

"I don't publish ethics, but I get it ethically, Jackie. However, I can't expect you to follow that. As with all flatfoots—"

"Shut up a minute. Is there anything else, anything, that you could add to what you've said?"

"Surely: 'You're welcome.' "

"For chrissakes, be serious. Listen, when you say the syndicate, you mean the S. S. Smith operation here on the Coast?"

"The same."

"From what you know about him, would you say he'd be likely to import independent talent?"

"Why, Jackie, you asking me?"

"Yes, I'm asking you! I'm after popular opinion, so to speak. I got my own data on Smith, but I'm just asking in general. So what do you say?"

"I say, 'Jackie,' I say, 'you're shouting at me again.' Your nerves, twittering from long inactivity and suppressed rage at failure, are beginning to show their frazzled little heads. No, I wouldn't say about S. S. Smith. In general, he might do anything. He's big enough to seem inconsistent in his doings."

"What kind of double talk you giving me? I got the distinct feeling you're getting tired of talking to me. What else do you know?"

"Honest, Jackie, nothing else."

"Come on, come on!"

"Honest! I got an idea, though. I got an idea you need a little relaxation. How about covering some night spots with me tonight?"

"Can't make it, Larry. I've got to hang around here. There're a few interviews and so on, then this lead you gave me I've got to check, and—well, I just can't."

"Jack Herron. This will be on me. My expense account. Come on, now, you just suffer from lead in your pants. What do you say?"

"I'm not a drinking man."

"Sure, Jackie. Uh—I bet you never did see a movie star in real life."

"The hell with movie stars."

"O.K., forget they're movie stars. They still got the most beautiful rear ends, the most monumental chests. I'm talking about the female ones, of course."

"No, I don't think so, Larry. Ah, when are you going, anyway?"

"Meet me at nine. At the paper. You know my office. And then we'll talk some more. Who knows, something might turn up during the night. I pick up the cu-rayziest items, you know."

"Don't I. O.K, Larry, at nine."

"So long, Investigator."

Before Herron left the office for the day he went to the communications room again.

"Nothing for me?" he asked the girl who was sorting message sheets at a long table.

"Nothing here," she said. "But let me check in the back."

She smiled at Herron and got up. He watched her walk the length of the room, paying close attention to the way her hips moved. But then he looked away, worrying about Chief Jones's answer to his teletype. Was he going to be pulled off the assignment? Better let Jones know about Larry's lead right away. Perhaps it did mean something.

Then he saw the girl come back. This time he watched her front move.

"Nothing yet, Mr. Herron.…Mr. Herron, I said—"

"Ah, yes, fine. Will you take something down for me, for teletype?"

"Of course, Mr. Herron."

She sat down and picked up pencil and message form. Herron watched her bare arm as she made date, hour, and name entries. She had a nice brown arm.

"The message, Mr. Herron?"

"Of course. Uh—where'd you get that nice tan so early in the year?"

"Santa Monica, the beach. It's not really so early in the year for us."

"Oh, I see. Very nice tan. You must tan beautifully. I mean, on the beach there."

She looked up at him with a light laugh, but didn't say anything.

"Ah, tell me. I have an assignment tonight, ah, involving nightclubs. Would you like to—can you perhaps come along? What I mean is, less conspicuous, you know, being a couple. Besides, I would very much like—"

"I'm sorry, Mr. Herron. It's real nice of you to ask me, but I'm married."

"You're married?"

"Why, yes. Surprises you?"

"Ah, oh, no, I didn't mean that. No surprise, actually. But a disappointment. Ha-ha."

She laughed too and looked down at her message pad again.

"Well, the message, then," he said. Herron dictated, not looking at her arm.

That evening he went out with Larry.

Chapter Eleven

"So I see you made a contact," said the Turtle. Then his eyes bugged out more than usual when he got a closer look at Catell. "Behold the Duke," he said. "Just get a load of the Duke in them fancy duds. Tonio, you musta made goodio. What happened?"

Catell dropped the cartons he was carrying on the bed and took off his new sports jacket.

"Put it back on," the Turtle said. "That neon shirt is kicking my eyeballs."

"Whaddaya talking about? It's California style, isn't it?"

"No, it ain't. You see anybody walkin' around like that who ain't a tourist or an actor or somethin'?"

"Well, anyway, I just got this one."

Catell sat down and lit a cigarette. The Turtle stood opposite, waiting.

"So give. What's the glad news?"

"No glad news, Turtle. I think I'm going to get someplace, but so far I've been roped."

"Roped? How?"

"I'm doing a job for that fat Smith guy. First the job, then the gold deal."

"So whaddaya kicking about? So you pick up some extra change plying your trade and also make a most evaluate contact and this you call roped!"

"Yeah, roped. Because I don't want no part of that syndicate and the way they run things. I need a free hand. I'm no soldier, you know, or a college kid getting a bang out of playing fraternity. That's what I'm talking about."

"Did you sign up for twenty years, maybe?"

"Maybe I did! I don't know who's gonna plan this heist or if it's any good, and maybe some ass I don't even know screws the works and I get it in the neck. So don't talk to me about that goddamn syndicate or I might even change my mind. Well, forget it, Turtle, I'm just jumpy is all. Here's your cut."

"My cut?"

"Yeah. Your share. I got paid five hundred on account There's over four hundred left. Take it already."

The Turtle took the money and stuffed the bills in his pocket without counting them.

"Thanks, feller. You an' me—"

"Cut the mush, Turtle. And now for some fun. Tonight you and me are going to hit the Pink Shell. Whaddaya say?"

"Man, you're stepping. You know what that place costs? I been in this town five years, off and on, and I only been hearing about the joint."

"Tonight we'll see it."

They went to the Pink Shell by taxi. After paying a fortune for the fare, they walked around the wide stucco building fronting on the ocean. There was a big moon up and a long pier reached far out over the black, rolling water.

"I hear they got parties down here sometimes. Private parties on the beach," the Turtle said.

"Too damn cold. Let's get inside outa this wind."

Like Paar's place, the Pink Shell was both a regular nightclub and a private club. But in this case the public part was no crummy roadhouse. White baroque columns supported the arch of a rose-colored ceiling. The walls were covered with pink satin, draped in fancy patterns, and stucco statues of naked mermaids flanked the shell-shaped booths along the walls. The mermaids all had pink nipples and red painted mouths.

"Like a dream," said the Turtle. "Just like a dream. Pinch me, Tonio. No, let Mabel do it." He watched the hostess come forward.

If a snake had legs, that's the way a snake would have walked. The hostess slunk up to them, carrying a little pink book in which reservations were marked.

"It may be difficult to find you a table," she said when Catell told her they had nothing reserved.

"Don't bother with this room," said Catell. "Too crowded. Something a little more private."

"I'm sorry, sir. Without—"

"Call Topper. Tell him Catell wants a space off to the side there, that low room over there."

The girl went to the wall phone and made a call. Then they watched her come back. She had a high, complicated coiffure, but the dress she wore was simplicity itself. High neck, long skirt, and sleeves coming to points over her hands. What recommended the outfit was the way it clung to the girl's body. She waved them to follow her and led the way to a side room.

"Tony, that dress!" The Turtle clutched Catell's sleeve. "That dress is better than skin."

"The Pearl Room, gentlemen. Miss Rosemary will take care of you."

Miss Rosemary could have been the other one's twin. Same hairdo, same body, same dress. Her face was a little different, but that wasn't the main attraction, anyway. Miss Rosemary led the way to a small table. There was a

pink tablecloth and just enough room for elbows and perhaps a glass or two.

"Two bourbons on the rocks," Catell said, and Miss
Rosemary drifted off, smiling.

"Tony, I think I'm too impressed to have a good time."
The Turtle spoke in a whisper.

When the drinks came, a waiter was carrying them.

"I'm sobering up already. Here's to you, Anthony."

"Mud."

They drank.

When they ordered their second round, a piano started
to crash out some chords and a rose light hit a curtain at
the end of the room.

"A floor show yet! They must have one of them stages
in every room here."

"Must be. Christ, look at that!"

The curtain whipped open with a fast swish and five
chorus girls, dressed like the belles of the nineties, came
tearing out on the small stage. Brass trumpets and drums
joined the piano, but that didn't drown out the girls. In
high-pitched voices they screeched a kind of ragtime
ballad about an evil baron and five poor sisters, all inno-
cent and beautiful till the baron came along. All the while
they kept bumping and grinding fast. When the refrain
came, they tore off their hats. A midget dressed like a
Turk rushed around to pick up the hats. Next refrain, off
came the gloves. Next refrain, the dresses. The midget
kept picking things up. Then the chemises came off. The
song got louder, the rhythm jacked up to a terrific pace.
Off with the corset. Practically naked, they shivered
themselves back and forth. Then the last refrain. With
crashing of trumpet, drum, piano, and high voices, they
ducked behind a skimpy screen that left their legs and

shoulders exposed. The music jumped once and stopped. In the silence only some rustling could be heard, legs and arms moving behind the screen. Then the loud tune started up again, frantic and harsh, and bras and panties came flying over the screen. With a last scream of the music each girl ducked from behind the screen into the wings of the stage. There was just a glimpse possible as they ran across the short open space.

"My, my, my," said the Turtle. "Oh, my, oh, my! Why wasn't I born a midget? My, oh, my."

Then the music changed to strings and sax. To a slow rhythm the girls came out again holding fans in front of them. The song was a tired thing now, something about five virgins no more, but another one already catching the black baron's fancy, another one pure and young, not knowing of the fate that lay ahead. At that point the rose light got dimmer and a white spot grew against the back curtain. It opened slowly and out walked Lily, Paar's cigarette girl. She half sang, half talked, moving up to the ramp with a slow swing of her hips.

Catell picked up the Turtle's half-full glass and poured it down.

"Christ," said the Turtle. "She can't sing, Tony."

"Shut up!"

"All I said—"

"Shut up!" Catell's voice sounded raspy.

Lily was standing still now, doing her lines, and her only movements were those made by her breathing. She was wearing a long, plain dress, all white, and like the things on the hostesses, the cloth held her body like a second skin. But Lily looked like no snake; Lily looked like a woman.

When her song was over the lights went dead. After a

minute they went on again, showing the stage empty.

Catell got to his feet. Then a smooth voice said:

"Leaving so soon?"

Topper was standing beside the table.

"I said, are you leaving already?"

"How are you, Topper? Nice club you got here," Catell said.

"And who's the runt with you?" Topper asked.

Catell sat down again and kneaded the fingers of one hand. "Topper," he said, "I want you to try to watch that tone of voice. You're talking about a friend of mine, and when it comes to crappers like you I don't mind getting my hands dirty messing you up."

"Now, now, Catell, that nasty, nasty temper of yours. I don't think Mr. Smith would approve of any of this. We should try and be friends. Don't you think so, Bugeye?" He turned to the Turtle.

Catell jumped up, but Topper had already stepped back and around the table. He stumbled against the Turtle, who hadn't said a word, but then regained his balance. With a bored expression he turned and left.

"Turtle, listen. I'm sorry about this and I promise you the sonofabitch will pay for it. Right now I'm trying not to make a commotion, but believe me, he's going to pay for this, Turtle. So—"

"Stop jabbering, Antonio. He's paid already, so let the poor sap go." The Turtle leaned back, looking disinterested.

"Turtle, listen, I mean it."

"Can that sentimentation, friend. And let poor Topper go. Like I say, he paid already." Turtle reached into his jacket pocket and showed the edge of a thick sheath of bills.

"Christ! Turtle—"

"Anthony, you are sentimentating again. Now let me finish."

From his breast pocket the Turtle pulled another handful of folded bills, letting just the edge of them show from under his hand.

"What did you do with the wallet? Are you trying to get us killed right here, you jerk?"

"Anthony, of what you speak, I know all about it. Now slosh another drink for yourself while I return the recriminating evidence."

"Why, you nut! How—"

"Quiet. I am an artist." The Turtle left the table.

Topper was standing near the archway of the room, greeting two men who had just walked in.

"Did we miss the show, Topper?" one of the men asked.

"You did, Larry, but why don't you catch the one in the Boudoir, or in the Shell Room?"

"Second best, Topper. I wanted my friend Jackie Herron to see Lily. Jackie, you oughta see Lily sometime, if only out of scientific curiosity. She doesn't do a damn thing, and you should see how it goes over. Topper, meet my friend Jackie."

Topper shook hands with the one called Jackie, but they didn't pay much attention to each other. Jackie seemed to be watching one of the hostesses, and Topper was watching Larry.

"There's nothing going on today, Larry. No celebrities."

"Topper wants to get rid of us, Jackie," Larry said, but Herron wasn't paying attention. He had been watching the backside of Miss Rosemary, and now he was watching her front.

"You want to be introduced?" Topper said.

"Oh, ah, why not?" Herron tried to look unconcerned.

"I'll tell you why not." Larry took Herron by the arm. "Because neither your expense account nor mine could take care of that situation. So, if you don't mind, Topper, we'll just walk around for a look-see and then breeze, eh?"

As they started to move, Topper bumped into the Turtle for the second time. The Turtle, looking apologetic, tried to fade back, but Larry spotted the maneuver.

"Hey, if it isn't the Turtle! Now, don't run, Turtle. Since when have you been admitted to the likes of this here pleasure dome?" He turned confidential. "Or is it strictly business, ha?" The Turtle looked as uncomfortable as a hung-up dog.

"So say something, Turtle. Listen, Jackie, this guy Turtle has a very interesting background."

"Larry—uh, Mr. Metcalf, I mean—I don't think—"

"Oh, shush yourself, Turtle. I wouldn't wash your old socks right here in public. I'm just chatting, you know, trying to make everybody feel at ease. So tell me, how are pickin's these days, Turtle?"

"I don't know what you mean, Mr. Metcalf. What you mean by pickin's, I mean."

"Just talking, Turtle, just talking. So come here and meet Jackie. Jackie, the Turtle; Turtle, the Jackie. Ah, you know the Turtle, Topper?"

"No. How do."

"Sure. And now, if you'll—"

"Don't go, Turtle." Larry grabbed him by the arm. "Why don't we chat a little longer? Like how's business and so forth?"

"What is your business?" Topper wanted to know.

"Then you *don't* know the Turtle!" Larry sounded full of happy surprise. "Well, now, the Turtle used to go by another name. And this is confidential, of course. Shut up, Turtle, I'm telling a story. He used to be a magician, Dippo the Short or something like that. How that guy could make things disappear!"

"Dippo? What kind of a crazy name is that?" Topper frowned.

"Yeah, Topper. Dippo the Short, wasn't it, Turtle?"

"So help me, Mr. Metcalf, you promised to lay off'n me."

"Never you mind, now, there's no harm done."

"If you'll excuse me, gentlemen," Topper said, and he stepped past them in order to greet another party.

They let him pass, looking after him. Larry said, "Watch him, Jackie, watch what he does now. Hey, you too, Turtle. Don't run off. Haven't you got any pride in your work?" Larry held the Turtle by one sleeve.

"What's he supposed to be doing?" Herron wanted to know. "I don't see a thing."

"You see it, don't you, Turtle, ha? Look, he's doing it now."

Topper had stopped at the entrance to the main room, and he was patting himself, as if he were hunting for a cigarette. Then he slipped his hand inside his jacket, looked in, and straightened up again. That was all.

"You mean he's looking for a smoke?" Herron said.

"Smoke! With your training, Jackie? I'm dumfounded."

"Was he looking for his wallet?" Herron looked at the Turtle with a little more interest.

"As the Turtle will tell you, Jackie, yes. He was looking for his wallet."

Herron started to grin. He looked down at the Turtle and said, "You little weasel, so you were—"

"Turtle, Jackie. Not weasel."

"So you were trying to lift his wallet, right here in front of everybody?"

"Now listen, you guys, all you're trying to do is get me in complications. If I told ya what's what you wouldn't believe it noways."

"You mean you did lift it? But—"

"Jackie. He didn't lift it. Didn't you see Topper pat himself? He found it."

"Well," Herron said, "I guess you can't always win, can you, Turtle?"

Larry noticed the look on the Turtle's face.

"Now you hurt his feelings, Jackie. You hurt his feelings and cast aspersions and disparagement—get those words, Turtle—on his professional standing. Tell him, Turtle."

"He won't believe me." The Turtle looked stony.

"So I'll tell him."

"Never mind, I'll tell him," said the Turtle. "I was returning the wallet, I was."

"You dumfound me, Turtle," Herron said.

"Well, if you don't mind—"

"No, you don't." Larry grabbed for the arm again. "First you buy us a drink, ha?"

"No, I'd rather not. In fact—"

"Perhaps you're broke, Turtle?"

"Larry! Are you disparaging my finances?"

"God forbid, Turtle. I wouldn't do such a thing. So come along, one and all. The Turtle is going to quench us."

"Naw, I don't think your friend here—"

"Turtle," said Larry, "let's not try stalling men like me and Jackie. You owe us a drink, don't you? Listen to me, Turtle, I'm now speaking with a significant voice: You owe us a drink, don't you? Because you owe your success to us, don't you?"

"What in hell you talking about, Mr. Met—ah, Larry?"

"Come on, Turtle. Don't tell me you gave Topper back a full wallet?"

"All right, dumfound you, I'll buy you guys a drink, and I hope you get aspersions from it."

Topper watched the three men from afar. When they sat down at the bar, he patted his breast pocket again. The wallet was there, plump as ever. If that little runt was a dip, even if he was a friend of Catell's— Topper didn't like any of the three men at the bar. Larry was a snooping nut, and with enough stuff behind him to be a real danger. That Herron character somehow didn't sit right, either. One of those characters you couldn't place. And the Turtle, a friend of that slime Catell—

Topper put his hand in his pocket and pulled out his alligator billfold. It was so stuffed that the flaps opened up in his hand.

Suddenly Topper's eyes got droopy, the way they had done when he had tangled with Catell in the machine shop. His color got darker, and his neck swelled out. Topper opened the billfold all the way. Folded inside there was a pink napkin.

When Topper got to the bar, only Herron and Larry were sitting together.

"Where's your friend, Larry?" Topper sounded smooth and unruffled.

"My who? Topper, you hit a sensitive spot there. I have no friends."

"That other guy, the runt. Where is he?"

"What I mean is, no *real* friends, Topper. You were saying?"

But Topper had turned and gone. He went around a corner to get to Catell's table. It was empty.

Back at the bar, Topper used the house phone, giving instructions.

"Oh, Topper, you looking for the Turtle?" Larry was leaning over the bar, waving an arm.

"Yeah. Your friend."

"He left, Topper. He left after buying us two of your most expensive drinks. Tell me, Topper, why do you charge—" but Topper had turned and gone again.

"Not very friendly," Herron said.

"This is nothing. Sometime you should introduce yourself as the cop you are, Jackie, if you want to study the ultimate extent of true unfriendliness."

Meanwhile Topper was walking down a service corridor. He was licking his lips and there was a mean wrinkle down the middle of his forehead. Footsteps sounded and one of his boys came around a bend.

"Well, where is he?" Topper said.

"Not a trace, Topper. I swear we looked everywhere. I think he musta—"

"Don't think, damn it. Find that dip. Find him, I don't care where, and bring him back. Alive. Just so he's still alive. Now beat it."

"Yes, sir. Another thing, the car's ready out back. That is, if you still want it,"

"Yeah, yeah, I want it. I'm getting Lily now. Have Rudy drive her home."

"O.K., Boss."

Topper walked up to a door that had a paper star glued to it and started to open it when he heard voices.

"Of course I remember you." It was Lily's voice.

Topper stopped, stiff.

"I'm glad," Catell's voice said.

Silence. Then: "And I remember you, it goes without saying."

"Is that why you came back?"

"You might say that. I came back for more."

"Of the same?" Lily's voice sounded amused.

"Don't kid yourself. I mean that you and me—"

"It's no good, Tony. This'll only mean trouble."

"Listen, kid. Maybe you're too young to know, though I doubt it, but it's worth the trouble."

"I don't know. I think you'd better go, anyway."

Catell couldn't make her out. Was she interested, was she just playing, or was she afraid? It could also be, with her wide-eyed face always looking a little vague, that Lily didn't have any feelings about this thing, one way or the other. Catell wondered how she'd look when she was excited. She must get that way sometimes.

"Leave the worrying to me, Lily. I got plans in this town, and one of the biggest of them is you. Lily, I'm not just playing around. I'm not just..." Catell's voice halted, getting nowhere. In the silence, he heard the door open. He spun around.

Topper walked in. "Go on, *Tony*. I might as well hear the rest. For that matter, you might as well finish what you had to say while you can." Topper had an easy smile on his face.

Lily blinked her eyes but there was no clear emotion on her face. Catell stood wide-legged, his face turning to sharp stone.

"Let's have it out right here and now," Catell said. "I didn't come here to get in your way. I came here after Lily, and no matter what gets in my way, I mean to have her. And I'd just as soon kill you, Topper, you and anybody else who gets in my way. I'm not trying to beat your time, either with Lily or with your boss. I just want what I want, and I'm going to get it, and I don't go for the kind of gaff that punks like you hand out."

Catell's voice had stayed on an even pitch, but he felt a

harsh excitement and a powerful certainty surge through him as he stood tensed, hands curled at his sides, his sharp face very still.

Topper gave the only answer he knew how to give. He reached for his gun. Before he had it out, Catell grabbed Lily's arm and swung her in front of him.

"Catell," Topper said, "how yellow can you get?"

Catell didn't answer.

"Catell, I'd just as soon shoot right through this dame to get you."

"Baby!" Lily's voice made a sound of surprise.

"Shut up! You think you're special? You think I wouldn't just as soon kick you over?"

Lily started to moan, but it wasn't so much because of Topper's words. Catell's hands, holding the girl in front of him, had dug into her arms like claws.

"Make him move, Lily." Topper stepped closer. "Make him move. Kick back."

But she didn't. She stood still, facing Topper and his gun. Then her head sank down and her knees bent.

"Drop her, Catell. Drop her or I shoot the both of you." Topper took another step forward.

But Catell didn't move. He knew that Lily hadn't fainted. He could feel the muscles in her arms tense under his hands. Then she kicked her foot, hard and swift.

It caught Topper square in the groin. He buckled slowly, his eyes rolling blindly in their sockets and his red mouth puckered. When Topper hit the floor, Catell let go of Lily's arms and reached down for the gun. Then he straightened up and took Lily around the waist.

"Thanks, baby," he said.

When he leaned over to kiss her cheek, she drew back

and hit him in the face. She didn't slap him; she hit him hard with a closed fist.

"For chrissakes! What in hell was that for?"

But Lily wasn't listening. She stood by the wall, her hands over her face, crying in a concentrated way. Catell shrugged and turned back to Topper.

"Can you hear me, punk?"

Topper opened his eyes and his face relaxed a little.

"Listen close, Topper. You touch Lily for this and I'll get you for it. I'll get you for it so you die in the end, but way in the end. And it's going to take time, Topper. You listening?" Catell grabbed the man's lapels and jerked.

"Stop it, stop it, you!" Lily, hands over her cheeks, stood by the wall, screaming.

"Lily!" Catell got to his feet. "What is it with you?"

"Stop it now, for God's sake stop it, you two!"

"You in love with this crud? What's—"

"I want you to stop this. I don't care what you do, but please, no more, please," and she ended with a sobbing mumble behind her hands.

Topper got to his feet slowly. He looked at Catell with a poisonous hate in his eyes, and there was slobber on his wet lips.

"Catell—"

"Shut up. You heard what I said?"

Topper didn't say anything, just looked.

"And another thing, Topper. Remember you and me are on the same team. I don't think *Mr.* Smith is going to like you very much if anything happens to me now. So keep your distance, Topper. Just another few days and I'll be blowing town. After that, anything you want to throw my way, throw it. And when it comes back at you, don't say I didn't warn you."

Catell put Topper's gun in his pocket and walked to the door.

"I'll be seeing you, Lily," he said. She didn't look up. He shut the door behind him.

He stopped for a moment to light a cigarette. There was movement in the room, feet shuffling. Catell could hear a dull smacking on flesh and Lily moaning. Then Catell walked on down the corridor and left.

"Jackie, this dullness dulls me. Let's you and me climb off these stools and go someplace else." Larry pushed his glass back and made ready to go.

"Why not hang around here, Larry? I might get to like it here." Herron kept watching Miss Rosemary move around.

"Come on, Jackie, up. I got to make the rounds yet. It's my bread and butter, and this place is a dud."

They got up and left because there was nothing going on at the Pink Shell.

Chapter Twelve

The tension was greater in Catell than he had ever felt it before. He stood at the open window of the Turtle's room, staring through the yellow smog where the sun was coming up. He didn't remember sleeping last night, just jumping up several times, fully awake. The Turtle hadn't come yet.

Catell didn't worry about the way he felt. He didn't think about the why, the how, or any of those things when it came to the state he was in. He didn't worry about the way Lily might feel, either. For all he knew, she hated his guts. For all he knew, she'd been doing daisy chains since she was ten. He didn't give a damn. He wanted Lily now, without question and without thought of consequence.

He put on his jacket. When his right hand came through the armhole he winced at the strange feeling in his hand The sharp pain of yesterday had gone, but there was an unpleasant dull pressure around the old cut. Catell looked at it and wondered at the pulpy, dry hole in his skin.

According to the old janitor at the Pink Shell, Lily lived in an apartment in Westwood. Catell took the bus down Wilshire, got out at the Village, and walked the rest of the way. He didn't remember ever feeling like this before, except perhaps that first time he ever did anything big. He had been fifteen and Joe Lenkovitch had promised him fifty bucks. Just jump in the car, drive it to the garage under the store where Lenkovitch had a paint shop, and collect the fifty bucks. When he'd first started the motor of the stolen car, he'd felt excited, crazy. The feeling stayed with him all the time he drove through town, wound around dark streets, and then pulled down the drive into the basement garage. He was so hopped up when he delivered it that he walked out without even asking Lenny for the fifty bucks.

There was a short hill up to the apartment house where Lily lived, and Catell felt winded when he reached the building. He was still breathing hard when she opened the door.

"I came to see you, Lily," he said.

She stood by the door with that open look on her face, showing nothing one way or the other. But Catell wasn't studying her face. She was standing in front of the light that came through the large glass doors of the sun porch, and there was nothing vague about the rest of her. Her shorts just reached the curve of her thighs. She was wearing a man's white shirt, the tails tied in a knot at her midriff, the folds of the material stretching up and over her breasts. When she finally moved, Catell saw she was naked under the shirt.

"I don't think you should come in, Tony," she said.

"Try and stop me."

"Tony, it isn't safe. I don't think—" Catell put his hand on the doorknob and slammed the door open. Then he stepped inside and pushed the door closed behind him. The spring lock clicked.

"Tony, he has a key. Topper has a key."

Catell ran his hands up and down Lily's arms, stroking gently.

"I hurt you last night?"

"A little."

"I'll make it up to you, Lily."

She didn't answer him, standing still under his moving hands. There was a short distance between them, just enough so he could not feel the touch of her breath. She stood quietly, only moving her tongue once, to moisten her parted lips. She breathed more deeply, never moving. Then Catell stepped back; his voice sounded squeezed when he said, "Like the first time, Lily. Go ahead."

She unbuttoned the front of the shirt, untied the knot. The thing fell to the floor. When she reached around to pull the zipper on the side of her shorts, Catell watched how her arm pushed the breasts together.

Then Lily was naked.

Catell curled his fingernails into his palms, trying to kill the tingling. One more second, he thought, one more second. Just reach out there, and then... Now there was a smile on Lily's face. Clearly, no question about Lily any more.

Her eyes widened, staring, and she moved as if to hide herself. Catell reached forward, lunging, and the world jarred with a screeching, searing flame of red that weaved, burst, and then sank sharply into itself, leaving nothing but a total dead black.

"I don't like this, Topper. I think you're making a mistake."

"I'm not asking you to think. Just drive this car and shut up."

"Boss, listen, I ain't never butted into your business before, but—"

"So don't start now, Nick. I'm warning you to shut up."

Nick didn't say any more. He concentrated on driving the car through the Santa Monica traffic, but he didn't feel right about the whole thing. With a slight twist he could see Topper's face in the rear-view mirror and the sight made his skin crawl. The face was pale, showing the red lips like raw flesh, and two ugly lines curved around the corners of the mouth. Nick couldn't make out Topper's eyes. They were closed, mostly, with only a wet glitter showing through the lashes.

When the car reached the end of Wilshire, Nick turned right on Ocean Drive. The sharp turn threw Topper to the left so that his head moved out of line with the mirror. Then Nick saw Catell lurch into his line of vision. Only the top of his head showed, sticky with blood.

The car straightened out and shot north. Topper pushed Catell back into the other corner of the seat by jabbing his knuckles painfully into Catell's ribs. Catell didn't seem to notice. He was still out.

"Reach me a light, Nick."

Topper took the car lighter and put it to his cigarette. When he was through the thing was still red, and slowly Topper pushed it into the limp man's neck. At first there was no reaction from Catell, but suddenly he started to twitch and a dry snore rattled out of his slack mouth. He didn't wake up, though.

"Take the light, Nick."

They drove in silence for a while.

"Lend me one of your fags, Topper?"

"When you gonna start carrying your own? Here."

"Thanks." After a deep drag Nick said, "Still going through with it?"

"Sure. Why?"

"Just asking."

"Let's have that pack." Nick handed it back. "And the light."

Topper lit his cigarette and gave the lighter back to Nick. A hot sun beat down on the highway, making the inside of the car like a steam bath. The windows stayed closed. Nick pulled his tie open by yanking the shirt collar away from his wet neck, but he didn't open the window. Topper didn't like to smoke with the wind blowing in his face.

After a while, Topper asked for the lighter again. He didn't like to light one cigarette from another.

"Boss."

"What?"

"Boss, listen. You nervous?"

"What's eating you, damnit? Spill it and shut up."

"Topper, now don't blow your top, but this is all wrong. You can't afford it, Topper, I know."

"Nick, what do I have to do to shut you up, damn it? Stop riding me or I'll—"

"Yeah, I know, Topper. You can do all kinds of things. But there's one thing you can't do, and I'm going to say it anyway. You can't buck Smith. If you rub out Catell, you're bucking Smith."

"Shut your crazy mouth and drive."

"Smith is counting on Catell for the job. If he finds out—and he will, you know—"

"To hell with Smith. To hell with your crazy talk, you stinking sonofabitch. Just do what I tell you."

Catell woke up with a sharp painful start, the light of the sun and the thick cigarette smoke stinging his eyes, his head a big bursting throb that jangled his senses at the slightest move. Topper sat next to him, a gun in his hand.

When the car turned into a dirt road Catell was just starting to think clearly. When the car bumped to a halt, hidden by the walls of a quarry, Catell knew for sure.

This was it.

"When you step out, Catell, don't stumble or anything. I'm right behind you." Topper jabbed the gun into Catell's ribs.

All three of them stood in the empty quarry, in the hot dust, looking at each other. The bright light made the shadows on their faces black and sharp, giving all of them the same expression. They stood without talking. The man who had driven the car started to push a stone around with his foot, not looking at anybody. Catell licked his dry lips, his brain a useless mess of pain, fear, and hate.

Then Topper started to smile. He held it so long that Catell thought time had stood still, or perhaps he was going out of his mind.

"Walk to the wall, Catell."

Catell walked. If Topper had told him to stumble, to hop on one leg, anything, he would have done it. He wasn't in a trance any more. His pain-sharpened senses raced for a clue, a sign, a hope, scanning the scene for that inevitable last chance.

"Stop."

Catell stopped.

"Turn around."

With his back to the baked wall of the quarry, Catell looked the way he had come. It wasn't very far. Topper stood with his gun in his hand. Then he raised the gun and took a careful stance and a slow aim.

"Hey, Catell, here it comes!"

Catell wished he had never come out of that trance. Even the harsh pain in his head no longer distracted him from the clear, real thing before him.

"Here it comes, Catell!" and the shot whipped out.

Spraying sand stung the back of Catell's neck before the true panic of the situation hit him. He wanted to scream, but there was no air in his lungs. He wanted to move, but his muscles were like glass, hard, near breaking.

"Guess I missed that time, eh, Catell?"

Never having finished—or even started—the scream of fear that choked him, that pushed his eyeballs from behind, he stiffened again when the gun moved up.

Again Topper shot.

"Seems I'm not doing so good, Catell, ha?"

The gun went down and Catell saw Topper change his stance. Time. Time to scream, to unwind, to melt like jelly in the heat. But nothing like that happened. The grip on Catell's control was frozen like ice. And then he began to tremble. The trembling hurt his head, his muscles, above all his head, but there was nothing to be done about it.

Topper laughed and shot again. The bullet hit close before Catell's feet. The trembling turned into a jagged, spastic horror of uncontrolled jerks, more intense each time a shot rang out.

Then there were no more shots.

"Catell, you can stop dancing. Hey, Nick, look at him. Christ! Hey, Catell, you can stop now. Take a rest while I load this gun. Catell, hey, look. Catell, I'm ready!

But Catell didn't respond. As his trembling died down his eyes became dull, and he stood, mouth open, breathing hard and deep.

"Come here, Catell. Come here!"

When Topper came up, cursing, Catell had gained a strange sense of detachment. He saw everything, he felt everything, but it didn't matter. The only thing that mattered was that Topper was still around, and that the time would come when Topper would be at the other end. Topper was just playing. There wasn't going to be any end yet. There was going to be time for Topper at the other end, because right now Topper was just playing.

The fist crashed into Catell's neck, making him fall to the ground. He could hear Nick's voice: "Don't muss him up, Topper. Remember about Smith." Catell knew he was getting a beating, but it didn't matter to him any more.

Later he woke on the beach, cold and sore, and the moon was up. He remembered everything, but it didn't really get to him. When he got back to the Turtle's room, he still felt the same about it: Topper had shot his bolt. Next it was going to be Catell's turn.

Chapter Thirteen

At four in the afternoon Catell was back in shape and ready to leave for Smith's place. First he had slept, then he'd gone to the Turkish bath, and then, after a hot meal, he hadn't felt so bad. His muscles were sore, but there was hardly a mark on him. Topper must have been using a newspaper. The cut on his head was tender, and a round burn on his neck looked an angry red, chafing under his collar. Only his hand worried him. The pulpy hole in the skin had puffed up, dripping a little, and the edges had turned dark. There was no real pain to it, just that strange ache.

The Turtle hadn't come home yet.

Catell picked up the gun he had taken from Topper in Lily's dressing room and checked it. There were six short bullets in the cylinder. The gun looked clean, had an easy action, and it fitted the hand well. There was no extra ammunition around, but Catell didn't figure he'd need it. He rarely carried a gun. If he had to use this one, six bullets were going to be plenty.

Catell went out, flagged a taxi, and gave an address in the Valley. Then he sat back and went over the whole thing again.

Meet at Smith's for last briefing. That would be at five. Drive to San Pedro with the team of three. Cruise Ruttger Road, where the Maxim Loan Company office was. Do that twice, and then stop two blocks down. That would be at eight P.M. Drop off Smiley, the guy who was going to help him. Drive another block and at eight-oh-five drop off the lookout. At eight-ten Catell would get out, carrying his suitcase, and walk the four blocks to the loan office. The driver was going to blow. At eight-twenty-five the lookout would stand in a doorway opposite Maxim's. Catell would enter the side door of the large office, and at eight-twenty-seven Smiley would join him. Besides having left the side door open, the inside man would have wedged the alarm bell, marked the position of two electric eyes, and cut the wires to all overhead fixtures. If something should go wrong, at least nobody could flood the place with light. Then Smiley and Catell would knock over the safe. It was an old-time job, with an alarm that cut in when the door cleared a contact. Catell was going to try to burn the hinges, tape the contact before it could cut in, and then pry the door back just enough so Smiley could squeeze through. Smiley was five feet tall and weighed eighty-one pounds. It shouldn't take too long. After Smiley handed out the bills, they'd leave the joint with the bills in the suitcase and let the loan office keep the tools. That would be at nine-ten. At that time the getaway car would pull up, having been parked two blocks down for the past twenty minutes. Now south, toward Laguna Beach. Halfway there, they'd gas up at a station in Corona del Mar. That's where they'd switch the suitcase to another sedan. The two men in that car would leave for Burbank, to deliver the stuff. Simple.

If they were interrupted anywhere along the line, it was every man for himself.

When the taxi made ready to turn off Van Nuys, Catell told the cabbie to stop. He got out, paid his fare, and walked five blocks to an address he hadn't given the cabbie.

The house sat far back from the street, behind a wall, a stretch of trees, and an open lawn. The big place looked empty, but the door opened as soon as Catell came up the broad steps.

"To the rear, last door on the left," said the maid who had opened the door. She was a maid only because that's what the uniform said. For a regular maid her legs were too good, her face was too much like a doll's, and her hair was too blonde.

Catell walked back. The room was a big, dark thing with leather chairs, carved tables, and a fireplace like a cave. A plaster stack of electric logs was plugged in there, giving off a steady red glow.

"You're prompt, Catell. Sit down." S. S. Smith waved his hand at Catell but stayed near the window, rocking on his heels.

When Catell sat down, the door opened again and two more men came in. One was a sullen kid with yellow hair and high cheekbones. The other was Topper. They sat down opposite Catell.

"Where's Smiley?" Smith wanted to know.

"Haven't seen him," said the kid with the cheekbones.

Topper looked across at Catell and grinned. Catell nodded. There was no expression in his face.

Then Smiley came in. He opened the door and held it for the girl in the maid's uniform. She carried a tray with five highballs, gave one to each of the men, and turned to go.

"But you just came, Rose," Smiley said. He held her arm.

"Let her go. This is business." Smith's voice was cold.

"Aw, come on, S. S. Just to look at. You know, an ornament. I ain't seen Rosie—"

"That's enough, Smiley. And you may leave, Rose."

They all held their highballs, not looking very comfortable, waiting for Smith to talk.

"You've gone over this deal enough times to do it in your sleep. If there are any questions, ask them now."

Nobody asked anything.

"All right. You know your places, you know your schedule. Catell and Smiley to knock the place over; Swensen, you're the lookout; Topper drives. I repeat this to make you understand one thing: Each has a job, one job and only one job. Do it, and the deal works. Muff it, and every other man is no better than a body minus a head. From now on, Catell takes over. His word goes for the rest of the operation. All right, Catell, it's all yours."

"There's just a few things. Once we hit that car, I don't want a lot of chatter. You know your jobs; there's no need to talk. Until you get on your stations, keep clammed up. Swensen, don't read a newspaper on your job. Looks too much like you got time to kill or just hanging around. And don't smoke. Same reason. Topper, any cruising you do, drive normal speed. Don't creep along, attracting attention, making it easy to remember you. Also don't ever gun the car. No two-wheel turns or any crap like that. Smiley, I'll talk to you once we're inside. That's all. Questions?"

No questions.

"All right, drink up and let's go. You got fifteen minutes."

Then they sat back and relaxed a little, but there wasn't much to talk about. Swensen offered Catell a cigarette and they said a few words. Topper went to the garage, turned on the motor of the limousine, and left it running. Smiley excused himself and disappeared down the hall. Smith smoked a cigar.

"How's it look to you, Catell?" Smith had walked over.

"O.K. Shouldn't be bad."

"Good. Think you can keep on schedule?"

"Should. If the dope on the safe is right."

"Good. All right, everybody. Time. Where's Smiley?"

Smith walked to the door when Smiley stepped in.

"Where the hell you been?"

"Time, S. S., I been making time."

When the four men passed through the front hall, Rose came the other way. Her apron was on crooked and her dress looked as if it didn't fit any more.

The kid who was going to be the lookout said, "They call him Smiley just to be polite. His real name is Mink. You get it, Catell? Mink." He laughed with a short, dry cackle.

Nobody talked on the way to San Pedro. Topper smoked one cigarette after another, drove the car well, and paid no attention to Catell, who was sitting beside him. Catell's suitcase was between his legs. When they cased Ruttger the first time, they didn't see anybody except a few pedestrians. When they drove past Maxim's the second time, there were a few pedestrians again. One of them had been there the first time.

"Slow down," Catell said.

"The time schedule—"

"Shut up, you sonofabitch, and slow down."

The short guy near Maxim's was the Turtle.

"Pull over."

"If you say so, Catell, but—"

Catell's left hand snapped across Topper's Adam's apple, making the man gasp with pain.

"Do only what you're told, Topper. Now pull up." The gun was in Catell's hand.

Catell opened the window and leaned out. When the Turtle came up, Catell said, "Wait for me two blocks down, fifteen minutes. All right, Topper, get going."

The rest of the drive went on schedule. Topper drove well, kept to himself. He looked bland.

When Catell came to the corner, the Turtle fell in with him. They walked, nodding and smiling at each other, and sometimes waving an arm.

"What's up, Turtle?"

"I don't know, Tony. I'm not sure. Christ, I'm sorry if I muffed something for you, but I couldn't get to you sooner. I knew you'd get here today, but I couldn't—"

"Whaddaya mean, couldn't get to me sooner?"

"Since that time at the Pink Shell I had a time shaking a couple of guys who was after me. Christ, did I have a time! Coupla Topper's men, on accounta that snatch I pulled on him, I think."

"That all?"

"Something else. I picked up a word something was cooking with you and Topper, so I tried to follow it up. Christ, did I have a time, with those torpedoes on my tail!"

"Hurry up, Turtle, what else?"

"I don't know for sure, Tony. Something about Topper getting to you. I couldn't get the details."

"Never mind. He got to me. That was yesterday. Now blow. I'm turning off here."

"No, Tony, that wasn't it. Yesterday wasn't it. I know he took you for a ride, but the word is there's a cross on."

"Frame?"

"Could be, Tony. Listen, this heist—"

"It's coming off as planned. Don't argue. When I cross over now, keep walking to the end of the block. Stay

there. After ten minutes, take the other end of the alley
next to Maxim's loans. After twenty minutes, the other
end of Ruttger. Watch for Topper and the sedan two
blocks down at nine. That's nine sharp, Turtle. He'll pull
up here ten minutes later. Got it?"

"Check."

"See the kid in the doorway, reading the billboard?
He's our lookout. Now blow."

The Turtle kept walking down the block and Catell
crossed to the alley. He turned once and looked at Swensen. Catell pointed with his finger at the Turtle, then
made a circle with thumb and forefinger. Swensen nodded.
Then Catell was at the side door and turning the handle.
No hitch. The door opened and Catell stepped inside.
For two minutes he stood in the dimness without moving.
Then Smiley came in. They stood another five minutes,
close to the door. Half a foot away, on a wooden railing
that ran from the side of the door to the middle of the
large room, there was a chalk cross. The two men dropped
to the floor and lay flat on their backs. Pushing with hands
and heels, they snaked their way along the railing, away
from the door. Once past the chalk cross, they got up and
walked.

"That eye was close to the door." Smiley was whisper-
ing. "Did you see it?"

"No. Just the cross. Good job. I guess we beat it
through. Nothing happened."

Just before they reached the large safe door, built flush
into the wall, they saw the second electric eye This one
didn't need a marker. The post with the light and lens
stood two feet from the wall to the left of the safe; the
post with the photoelectric cell was opposite, on the right
of the safe.

"Man, that's close." Smiley wiped his forehead.

Catell was sweating too. He had been dragging the heavy suitcase and the hand with the sore was throbbing. He didn't know whether he was nervous about the job, but he didn't feel so good. Almost feverish.

"That eye's too close, Smiley."

"You're telling me! The diagram said eight feet."

"That's what comes from not doing your own casing. That jerk who mapped this layout is going to be one sorry-looking bastard."

"Whatcha gonna do?"

"I gotta figure this. It's risky, but I could work inside two feet. No good, though. Once that door falls, the beam's cut."

"Jee-sus!"

"Open that bag, Smiley."

"O K. Now what?"

"There's a pencil flashlight in the pocket. Take it out. Now turn it on. Got it? The button, stupid, the little button. Now step close to the eye, point the light at it, and slip the flashlight up in line with the beam. But be ready to run, Smiley. I'm going to cut my hand through the beam back here, and if you hear a click in that thing, bolt! Understand? Fast now, go!"

Smiley slipped the flashlight in line with the eye fast, but steady. Nothing happened.

"Hold it now, Smiley. Here I go," and Catell swung his hand through the beam from the post

They listened tensely, Catell feeling the cold sweat run down his back. He shivered. No click.

"Once more, Smiley. Here goes."

Catell stepped into the beam. No click.

"It works. Now listen, Smiley. You'll have to hold that

thing from here on. I don't care if your hand drops off, but keep that light steady."

"Got you, Catell. Get to work, and good luck."

Catell pulled his tools closer and laid them out in a small half circle. After a swift study of the door, he changed his mind about the hinges and went to work on the tumblers. He stuck chisels, hammer, and probes in his pocket. Then, standing close to the door, he went to work on the lock with a drill.

"Keep looking out the window now and then, Smiley."

Catell worked without pause.

"How's your arm?"

"Dead. You getting anywhere?"

"Little more. Just keep that light steady."

After a while Catell put the drill down and used the chisels. The lock cover and a few disks came off. Then he went to work on the tumblers. Catell's movements were deft, sure, but he kept shaking his head.

"How's the arm?"

"Let's not talk about it. What I wanna know is are we gettin' anywhere?"

"I'm fixing the tumblers. It's going O.K."

"Whyn't ya use the soup?"

"And trip the alarm? This job wasn't laid out that way."

"Well, they tell me you know your stuff. But when you're through, don't pat me on the shoulder. My arm might drop off."

"Not much longer, Smiley. Keep it up."

There was silence for a while. Catell, working mostly by touch, started to swear under his breath.

"What's eatin' ya?"

"This whole goddamn job was laid out wrong. That's what comes from not doing your own casing. Whose cockeyed idea was it to burn this door through, anyway? This job should have been done by rewiring the alarms, cutting in on the timing circuit, and then knocking the safe over any way at all. But this horsing around with a live alarm contact— How's your arm?"

"What arm?"

"Anyway, looking at this place now, I would've knocked it over in the daytime, somehow."

"And shoot the place up? That's old-time stuff, Catell."

"Not the way I do it. Uh, I think— Here she comes, Smiley!"

There was a last click inside the tumbler chamber and then Catell spun the wheel. The large bolts slid back into the door with an oily swish, making the door swing free on its hinges. Catell jumped fast, catching the door before it swung out of its frame.

"That goddamn live contact. That sonofabitchin' live—"

He leaned against the door, sweating. "And this lousy door couldn't have been hung straight. No, they had to hang it so it swings open."

"Whatcha gonna do now, Catell?"

"I'll yank that desk over, to hold the door. Then I'll try burning part of the flange so I can slip through the crack and get that contact. And it better be where they said it was. Else we could be burning around here all night."

"How in hell you gonna get a desk without that door swinging open on you?"

"Yeah, how? I'll stay close up to the door. You move out of the beam and get the desk. That'll spell you, too. How's that?"

"Fine. Aren't ya gonna ask can I move my arm?" Cautiously Smiley got out of the way of the beam.

"One more thing, Smiley. If it clicks, jump and we open the safe as is. We'll grab some lettuce and the hell with that door alarm. I figure we're safe for about four minutes. O.K.?"

"O.K."

No click.

Smiley got up, groaning, rubbing his arm.

"What time is it?" Catell asked.

"Eight-forty-five. Can you make it in time?"

"Don't worry about it."

A few minutes later Smiley had edged a desk up to the beam, and Catell, still leaning against the safe door, was getting down to the floor to pull the desk up close. Smiley was starting to maneuver the flashlight into line with the photoelectric cell.

"Tell me when," Catell said.

"There's a guy by the front windows," Smiley said.

"Stay put. May be nothing."

The shadow against the window moved away while the two men lay on the floor, immobile.

Then the side door opened. It opened fast and shut fast.

"Relax, Tony. Turtle speaking."

"Stay where you are."

It was dark enough in the large office so that distant objects were hard to make out.

"How much change in my pocket, that first day in the bar?"

"Ninety-eight cents."

"O.K., Turtle, but don't move. They got electric eyes up."

"Tony, something's up."

Smiley's hand with the flashlight made a short jitter.

"Topper didn't show up, Tony. I waited four minutes, no car, no Topper."

"What is this?" Smiley's voice was shaky.

"You sure, Turtle?"

"Positive. Two blocks down, no car, four minutes late."

"A frame! Smiley, move out of the beam and beat it. I'll hold the safe till you get to the door. Go!"

In the silence of the dark room there was only the harsh breathing of Catell, leaning against the safe, and the sound of Smiley scraping across the floor where the other electric eye was.

They came in from all sides. Four of them burst through the front door, scattering behind desks and balustrades; four others swarmed through the side door, knocking the Turtle into the beam of the eye, stumbling over Smiley, who was still on the floor.

The alarm went off. The big bell over the front entrance started a dull rattle, getting sharper all the time. The wedge in the bell wasn't holding. The men at the side door had grabbed Turtle and Smiley, and a voice from the front yelled, "Hands up and walk out slow. The whole place is sealed."

Somebody flipped a switch, but the lights didn't go on.

Catell rolled away from the safe into the shadows of the back, and the safe door swung open slowly. There was a moment's complete silence as the light from inside the safe grew with the movement of the door. Then shots. Twice, four times.

"Cut it out, up front! We got two of them here."

"Parker, that you?"

"Yessir. We got two here. Wait'll we get the light."

"They don't work."

"Down, everybody. Here comes the flashlight."

One beam cut through the darkness, then two, three.

"Parker?"

"Yessir."

"You and Litvinoff take the prisoners outside. Lobos, bring a flood through the side. Chester, you get one from the front. The rest stay down."

They flooded the place with light, finding tools, Smiley's cigarette stub, an empty suitcase, a desk moved out of place, and the safe open. Then they gathered outside to look at the prisoners.

"We got these two, and one from across the street."

"Find anyone else inside?"

"Well, there were only supposed to be three."

"Guess this is them."

"What's your name?"

"I wanna see my lawyer!"

"What's yours?"

"Florence Nightingale."

"Yours?"

"Catell."

"Tessman, what was that name in the report?"

"Catell."

"Guess that wraps it up. Take 'em downtown. Parker, Lobos, you stay here. All right, boys, move it."

At eleven o'clock that night, Catell moved slowly out of the storage room and back into the main office. Lobos sat up front, smoking in the dark. Parker sat by the desk at the side door, his head on his arms, snoring. The cold draft from the door woke Parker with a start, but by then Catell was half a block away. He got to Burbank three hours later.

Catell paid the taxi and walked up to the dark machine shop. At the back a hair of light was visible through a scratch in one of the painted windows. There were two cars at the side. One was a fish-tail convertible; the other was the getaway car.

The guy that stopped Catell inside the shop recognized him and let him pass. Catell walked past the machines, through the windowless room, and opened the door to the inner office without knocking.

"—is a funny sort of timing, Topper," Smith was saying.

"But I saw them, Mr. Smith. I saw them—" And then Catell stepped inside the room.

Smith, leaning back in his chair, rolled the cigar around in his mouth. He looked at Catell, never changing his expression. It was calm, level, and just slightly interested. But Topper jumped.

"Why, you—how—" Controlling himself, he took a deep breath and said, "I see you made it, Catell."

"Yeah."

"How—what I mean is, did they follow you? Did you come alone?"

"Alone. Except for you, Topper."

"You trying to be funny, Blue Lips?" Topper got up slowly, his eyes slits and his neck swelling over the white collar.

"Not funny, Topper. Serious."

And while Smith sat in his chair, hands folded over his paunch, Catell's hand whipped out, grazing Topper's drawn lips. Topper had caught the jab with a fast block, and that was his mistake. With his full weight behind the punch, Catell, pivoting a half turn, rammed his other fist into Topper's stomach. The man doubled over, gasping, when Catell fired a roundhouse at the contorted face. Something cracked, and through split lips three front teeth jagged out.

Topper crashed sideways across the desk, pushing phones and papers to the floor. Smith got up and stepped back. He was holding the cigar between his teeth.

When Topper kicked his leg out, catching Catell on the chest, he tried to follow the kick with a fast turn that would bring him back to his feet. But Catell stepped back and pulled. Holding on to Topper's foot, he twisted and pushed. Topper slammed to the floor, screaming, one leg doubled over at a crazy angle. Then Catell knelt down over his chest.

Two minutes later he got up, leaving the ruined man curled on the floor.

"Do you carry a gun, Catell?" Smith came out from behind the desk; flicking some ashes on the floor.

"It belongs to Topper."

"Give it to me." Smith put out his hand.

Catell handed over the gun. Smith took it by the grip, and without seeming to aim he pulled the trigger. Three close shots crashed out and Topper twitched once, twice. Then he lay still.

"Too bad about Topper," Smith said. "Valuable man."

Then he walked around the puddle of blood on the floor. He pulled open a desk drawer and handed Catell two bills.

"Here's your thousand. Got a way home?"

"No."

"Take the limousine. And call me in a day or two."

"So long."

"See you, Catell."

That night Catell didn't go back to the Turtle's room. He drove to Westwood and parked the car a few blocks from Lily's apartment.

She opened the door for him, smiling a little. He could feel her warm body through the thin robe she was wearing. Walking to the bedroom with her, he could hear the fever pounding in his ears. A hysterical tension trembled through his body, making objects change shape before his eyes, plucking at his muscles.

They sat on the bed, and then his head sank into her lap. She hummed to him while he moaned into the cloth of her robe.

Chapter Fourteen

"I see nothing but gloom," Smiley said. "I see gloom turning the corner, bearing poisonous grub."

The police guard came up to the cell. Balancing a tray in one hand, he started to fumble with his keys with the other.

"Lemme give you a helping hand, Inspector. You hold the tray and I'll just—"

"Keep your hands off, Short Stuff! Maybe you think I'm stupid or something?"

"You're gettin' warm, Pop. You're gettin' real warm."

The guard stepped back and put the tray on the floor. When he raised himself, the exertion had turned his bald head a shiny purple, and he puffed air through his white mustache.

"Nature is cruel," Swensen said from the back of the cell. "Look at all that gorgeous hair under his nose, and nothing but bare rocks on top."

"You guys don't shut up I'll take the food back," said the guard.

"And eat it yourself?" Smiley asked.

"He's bluffing," Swensen said. "He come to poison us good and proper this tune. All this threatening is just a bluff."

"Let's see ya eat the stuff, Pop. I dare ya."

Mumbling through his mustache, the guard unlocked the cell door. Then he stepped back to pick up the tray, but stopped halfway down, grunting when he straightened up again.

"One of you guys come out here and pick that tray up."

"So's you won't be blamed for the consequences? Swensen, whaddaya think of old Pop now? Pretty sharp, this switch, eh?"

"Pretty sharp. Experience, I'd say."

"Whaddaya say, Tur—uh, Catell? Ya think we should do this thing for Poison Pop?"

"Give 'im a thrill, Smiley. Go out there and make a break for it."

"Come on, you nuts." The guard sounded querulous. "One of you come out here and pick up that tray."

"All right, men. When I give the signal, we rush him. One, two—"

The old man started to look confused. He stepped back.

Smiley said, "Good thing I can't count to three, Pop. It saved your life."

Then he stepped out of the cell and brought the tray back in.

"Knock on the bars when you're done." The guard was locking the door. "Knock on the bars and I pick up the tray."

"Get that," Smiley said "How's he expect us to knock on the bars, us dead from poisoning and layin' here stiff?"

"Buncha nuts," said the guard, shuffling off.

"Poisoner!"

They started to eat, laughing about the old man and making small talk. But they didn't feel right. They didn't feel right about being caught in a double cross.

"That Catell sure got a friend in you, Turtle. You realize what this means?"

"That's O.K. I been in stir but twice. Builds character, I always say."

"Yeah? I rather be without character," Smiley said. "Got a smoke?"

"Won't be much for the Turtle," Swensen put in. "What are they going to charge him with, lying to an officer of the law?"

"Associating with bad company. It's us they got over a barrel, Swensen. I get faint just thinking about it."

"Smith'll come through. I've seen him come through before. So you get a few years, rest up. You know."

"Swensen, for chrissakes, don't talk like that. Me, I'm a vital boy. I can't stand being locked up someplace."

"Whaddaya yammering about? You had Rosie yesterday. Look at us with nothin' to give us strength."

"Ah, Rosie. Such a friendly, friendly girl."

"Listen to that mush," Swensen said. "And I bet he don't even remember her face or the color of her hair."

"I ain't in the habit of remembering broads by unimportant details, Swensen."

"Oh, Christ. A jump artist. Wait'll they get you up to—"

"Catell. Up front." The police guard opened the door.

"But we didn't rattle the bars yet, Pop. Look," and Smiley held his plate up. "We ain't finished yet."

The Turtle got up and, stepping over Swensen, went to the open door.

"Fare thee well, men. And whilst I'm off to the torture chambers, fear not, for Pop here will be with youse."

"Come on, Catell, get a move on."

They walked down the corridor that led to the door and the precinct desk.

"Keep in touch," Smiley called. "You're O.K."

They put handcuffs on the Turtle and put him in a

police car. Then they drove him downtown, to the office of the FBI. The Turtle didn't say anything during the long ride. He didn't think that funny talk would make any difference any more.

Herron closed the folder, left his desk, and walked across the hall to the room they used for interrogations. There was a table in it, a water cooler, and a few chairs. On the wall was a two-year-old calendar with a big picture on top. It showed some kids jumping around in the water of an old swimming hole. A sign said, "No bathing."

Herron sat down on the table and lit a cigarette. His palms were wet and he sucked on his cigarette with nervous puffs. Then the door opened. Two officers and the Turtle came in.

"Here he is, Herron. Friendly as all get-out."

They unlocked the handcuffs and one of the men sat down at the table with a pad and pencil.

"This is supposed to be Catell?" Herron swallowed hard a few times and stared at the Turtle. "You mean this guy is Catell and just a few days ago I shook hands with him in a nightclub not knowing he's the guy I've been chasing all over the country?"

The Turtle looked down modestly.

"Sure it's Catell. And like the tip said, we caught him red-handed, knocking over that safe."

"Have his prints been taken?"

"Sure. Last night yet."

"Did you run them through?"

"No, but we will, if you want. Shall I get them started on it?"

"I wish you would, Parker. And let me know right away."

When Parker closed the door behind him, Herron got

off the table and walked around the Turtle, looking him over.

"I must say—uh—Catell, you don't look much the way I figured. You don't look much like your pictures, either."

"Couldn't have been a very flattering likelihood," said the Turtle "You know how them mug shots distract a guy's personality."

"Yeah. I guess. Tell me, Catell, how's your health been lately?"

"Lately? Fine, till yesterday."

"Yeah? Then what?"

"Well, it's like this: There was this guy they call Poison Pop; old geezer runs the clink at the Twenty-ninth Precinct in San Pedro. Now, soon as me and the boys—"

"Never mind. All right, Catell, let's cut out the bull and get down to cases. I guess you know we got you dead to rights this time and anything you do to stall the investigation can only make things worse. You understand that?"

"You mean worse than life? What, I ask, can be worse than life?"

"Where's the gold, Catell?"

"What gold?"

"When did you see it last?"

"See who?"

"Dick, you got that down? Catell, every attempt to stall this investigation will be held against you And just to get things straight, it might interest you to know that we are preparing a charge of assault with intent to kill. One of the guards at the university isn't doing so hot."

"Listen, Herron, you I can do without."

"Now you listen, Catell—"

"Catell? You talking to me, Herron? Because if you are, Buster, you got the wrong man."

Herron didn't say anything for a moment. He watched the stenographer finish his entry.

"That's the name you gave when arrested."

"That's the name *they* give *me* when I was arrested. For what, I know not. And now, if you please, who is Catell?"

"What's your name?"

"Who's Catell?"

"Listen, you. What I said before about co-operation still goes, no matter who you are. What's your name?"

"I wanna lawyer."

"All I want is your name, for chrissakes. You can give me your name without fear of self-incrimination, can't you?"

"You wouldn't say that if you knew what my handle was."

"What is it?"

"Egbert."

"Egbert? Egbert what?"

"Egbert the Terrible."

"Oh, for chrissakes!"

"I useta be a wrestler. They gimme the handle on account—"

"What you got, Parker?" The door had opened and Parker came in with papers in his hand.

"They don't match up, Herron. This guy ain't Catell."

"Didn't I tell ya, Mr. Herron? Didn't I just—"

"Aw, shut up. So who's this guy, Parker?"

"Local dip. Two minor convictions."

"And his name?"

"Turtforth. Egbert Turtforth. And get this: Used to be a specialty wrestler called Egbert the Terrible. Then for a while he was a magician with—"

"For the lovamike, get out of here. Hold him under

your own charges, drop him in a well, I don't care what. Dick, let's go. Wait till Jones hears about this. Christ, I can just see him now."

They walked across the hall to the large room where Herron's desk was.

"One blind alley after another. One funk after another. So help me, Dick, I don't think there is such a guy as Catell. I think this whole thing is nothing but a sly way of testing a man's sanity. Did you ever hear such a name as Egforth?"

"Egbert. Egbert Turtforth."

"All right, all right. And I bet you can read that name backward and get a valuable clue on how to win a box top free. I have a good mind right now—"

"You're wanted on line three, Herron." An agent at one of the desks was holding the phone, waving at Herron to take the call at his own desk.

Herron picked up the receiver. "Agent Herron speaking, may I help you?"

It was a woman's voice. It was a slurry voice that nevertheless made no attempt to disguise itself. "Hi, you Herron? Listen, I bet you haven't found my boyfriend Catell yet, have you? Well, it's time you got a little help around here. Wanna meet me?"

"Who's this calling? Your name, please."

"I'm in the Lifeboat, Beverly and La Cienaga, you know. You come on over, Mr. Herron. Ask for Selma."

Chapter Fifteen

When Catell woke in the morning, he remembered the way the night had started. He turned, leaning on his elbow. Lily was asleep there, her naked back a breathing curve. Catell remembered the rest of the night and felt better.

For the next five days they lived together, seeing no one, needing no one.

"I've never had it like this," he said. "Never in my life."

"Me neither," she said.

"That's because you're so young," he answered.

They ate out of cans, and Catell boiled coffee. Lily didn't know how to cook.

After two days they left the apartment and drove to Santa Barbara. During the day they lay on the beach; at night they stayed in a motel near the pier. It had two tiny rooms, fixed up like a home. Lying in bed at night, they could hear the surf; if they sat up they could see the slow roll of the breakers on the long, empty beach. The little ruffled curtains would move in the breeze.

"Let's play house," Lily said.

"We can't. You don't know how to cook."

"You hungry?"

"Nope."

"Then why're you talking about cooking?"

"Because you said that about playing house."

"I may not know how to cook, but I know how to play house." Lily smiled and let herself fall back on the bed.

There was nobody in Santa Barbara that they knew or that bothered to know them. Either way, they wouldn't have paid any attention. On the beach they lay in the hot sun, watching the play around them, not caring to join in.

"See those kids with the ball, Lily? High-school kids."

"They are?"

"Yeah. They're your age."

"Maybe. But not really," and Lily stretched in the sand, like a cat rubbing her back, smiling at Catell with a slow sideways look.

Catell suffered only in the evenings, or early in the mornings. None of his wounds had healed, and sometimes he felt weak, shivery, his body like a rag doll soaked in water.

"How long have you been like this, Tony?"

"I don't know. A long time, it seems."

Lily bandaged his hand; the gauze became stained quickly. And once, in the waves, his body froze with a sick terror, a steel vise cramping his chest, and the breath stuck in his throat like a solid thing. This he never told Lily, but the rest of the day he kept still, lying flat, sweat breaking from his pores with each movement.

Sometimes he thought of his gold; each time the hard will that dominated all his acts flashed up like a blinding flame, forging his doubts, his pains, even his pleasures into a sharp steely point, like a weapon. The new start, the new life, the big time. Lily. Did any of this exist without Lily? The gold had been there before Lily, and all his sudden strength that came on him suddenly like a cramp, that too had been with him before Lily. But all this, no different now than it had been before, existed now because of the girl—the woman he had found.

Lily had never spoken of such things. Her face was

open and seemed to say nothing, and she gave her body without gesture. Lily had happy days with Catell.

When they left Santa Barbara they moved into an apartment in Santa Monica. Then Catell called Smith.

"I have an office downtown," Smith said. "The Western Development Company. Look it up in the book. I'll expect you tonight at eight."

Lily went to the club to do her job, and Catell went downtown.

The place looked like any other office that used more than one desk. There was a railing with a swinging gate, there were several desks and filing cabinets and a switchboard. In the back an office was set apart by frosted glass. The place looked empty.

When Catell started through the swinging gate, the office door in the back opened and a goon with a face like a tomato came out.

"He's waiting for ya. Step right in," and the goon came past Catell and sat down at the switchboard.

Smith looked as he always did, rotund, a little jovial, his mouth busy on a cigar.

"Nice tan you got. Sit down, Catell, sit down."

Catell sat.

"And how's the little Lily?"

"She's— Why do you ask?"

"Just polite, Catell, just a polite inquiry."

"She's fine. You know why I'm here, Smith, so let's—"

"Of course. The gold. What do you think we ought to do, Catell?"

"What's there to think? We made a deal, we set the price, and this is it. Where do you want it and when? That's all there is to do, Smith."

Catell had started to raise his voice, but he controlled

himself. He saw a speck of dust on his pants and brushed it off with a short movement. "Our agreement stands, Smith. You're not dealing with a punk."

Smith exhaled noisily, letting the sound die down. Then he leaned back and looked at the ceiling.

"You say we have a deal on, Catell, and you are right. You did a job and I paid you. I paid you even though I didn't make a cent on that heist. In fact, it's costing me. Would you like to know how much it's costing me? However, that's neither here nor there. And the fact that you couldn't deliver is certainly not your fault. Nevertheless, the fact remains that the job did not come off."

"Just a minute, Smith. Before—"

"Please let me finish. You and I have a deal. That stands. I'm not trying to pull out, Catell, because that's not the way I work. But I'm asking you to stand by the terms of our agreement, just as I do. You've got to deliver."

"You blaming me for that fluky setup?"

"Certainly not. And those to blame have been dealt with. You were present on one of the occasions yourself. I am suggesting, in all fairness to both of us, that you go along with me once more. I have—"

"I don't operate that way, Smith. When—"

"I realize that, Catell. I realize the last operation cramped your style, there were holes in the planning, and I certainly didn't get the benefit of your talent. The next time, all that will be corrected. I want you to be in on the planning, you can do your own research, and I'll give you a percentage of the take."

"You have it all worked out, haven't you, Smith?"

"I have."

And Catell knew there wasn't anything he could do about it.

For a moment the thought made him see red. A thousand acrid hates rose in his throat. He closed his eyes, trying to control the fine trembling that crept through his body. He took a harsh breath. Watch it, Catell. You're getting like a hophead taking the cold turkey. Hold on, for the sake of—for the sake of everything. Why am I cracking now? The knowledge of his strange new weakness drove fear into him.

"Is anything wrong, Catell?"

He opened his eyes, face still. "Nothing, Smith. Too much sun, I figure. Nothing's the matter," and then his strength came back. There were small beads of sweat on his forehead, but he was himself again.

"I was just thinking, Smith. I was thinking you're right."

"Good. We'll talk about the details some other time. In general, it's the same operation as the last. There's a little resort up in the Sierras, small but expensive, where they run a sizable gaming room on weekends. You'll go up and have a look yourself. I'll give you a flat three thousand plus a percentage. We'll go over that the next time. This will definitely be your last commitment—if you wish— and we'll complete the rest of our affairs as soon as this is over."

Smith opened his wallet and took out three bills. "Fifteen hundred on account. Take it."

Catell picked up the money and stuck it in his pocket. Then they shook hands, Smith making a brief smile. When Catell was at the door, Smith said:

"Before I forget it. There was a call for you. A woman by the name of Selma."

"What!"

"The past, apparently, rearing its head, eh?"

"What did she want?"

"Nothing. I took the message, because she came well recommended. Our friend Paar gave her my number."

Catell walked back into the room "Why did she call?"

"She said to tell you she had arrived in town. And you should give her a ring at the Empress Arms."

"That all?"

"Yes. I'm not sure whether she was asking you or telling you. Why, Catell, you look almost human!" Smith gurgled a laugh and watched Catell's face turn glum. "Ah, I don't often do this, Catell, but would you care to talk about it?"

"There's nothing to talk about. I was just surprised for a minute."

"I noticed that. Sit down, Catell. Here, have one of my cigars."

"Thanks, I don't smoke cigars. Anyway—"

"Sit down, Catell."

They sat for a moment while Smith unwrapped a cigar for himself.

"I'm not concerned with anything in your life, Catell, except insofar as it affects your work in my organization. Please understand that. Now, just as I cannot tolerate a squealer in my work, I cannot tolerate the kind of problems that some men seem to have with women. I don't like messes, Catell."

"You're going a little far, aren't you, Smith?"

"I don't mean to. It's true, though, isn't it, that this Selma is a lush?"

"Would you believe it, Smith, I don't know. Selma was a dame I knew about ten years ago."

"How about Detroit?"

"Nothing. I'd just been out of stir a short while."

"Ah, I don't mean to sound superstitious, Catell, but the man who lived with Selma—Schumacher, I think— and the man who was with Lily, they are both dead now."

"I don't follow that. If you're not superstitious—"

"I'm not. Only some men, for vague reasons, unknown reasons, some men have a way of concentrating disaster around themselves, and it might be that you—and you'll admit there is nothing average about you—that you could easily—"

"I don't get any of that crap, Smith. I'm a guy like any other guy who knows what he wants and does all he can to get it. I've had my share of kicks, sure, but I'm as careful as the next guy." Catell sucked on his cigarette, hard. "Especially now," he added, and tossed the butt to the floor.

"Uh, now?"

"Yeah, now. I'm no spring chicken, Smith. It's time I made good and found something solid. I haven't got time to horse around. One, two solid jobs and I'm off this racket. I got some playtime coming to me and I mean to have it."

"Speaking of playtime, are you including Lily in all this?"

"I'll tell you this much, Smith: She isn't playtime. Let's just leave it at that."

"I'm sorry if this riles you, but, as I have said before, my only intent is—"

"Yeah, I know. Commercial."

"And that's why I cover all angles, Catell. Of course, I'm glad to see that you are serious-minded, and that your attitude is sober. But that's why I'm wondering. Don't you think Lily is a little young, uh, for you?"

Catell got up and went to the door without answering. Then he turned and said, "I'm forgetting you asked that, Smith. And remember, don't pump me again. You and me, Smith, we don't discuss Lily. Understand?"

Smith shrugged his heavy shoulders and turned the swivel chair the other way.

"Don't forget your message," he said to the opposite wall. "You're supposed to call this Selma."

Catell stepped through the door and slammed it behind him.

He took the Freeway to Hollywood and then cut over to Sunset. He turned on Vine, parked the car, and walked back to the corner.

The corner of Sunset and Vine was crowded with characters. Professional characters, unintentional characters, and the plain crazy variety. There was the guy who once had the bad luck of writing one hit song, and nothing since. There was the slob who had another deal on and he was bending somebody's ear about how the deal was hot. A high-stacked blonde was wailing for the light to change, looking busy and detached in dark glasses. Tourists hustled around in pairs, all atwitter with free passes to a TV broadcast. Catell saw them line up like sheep in front of CBS, all looking very much alike with cameras, Hawaiian shirts, and health shoes.

With nothing else to do, Catell walked into an ice cream parlor and sat down. He ordered Pistachio Delight, which came in a clifflike arrangement and smelled like perfume. He hated ice cream, but the glass dish felt cold in his hands, and he held on to the bowl as if it could draw the waves of fever out of his bones. Catell felt sick.

From where he sat, the night didn't look like night. An

unnatural glare covered the street, making harsh black shadows. Catell lit a cigarette. After a few drags he pushed the butt into the wet mess in his ice cream dish, where the cliffs had turned into a soggy bog, and went outside.

Catell wasn't the only one just standing around in the street, but he was the only one who wasn't rushing. Another hour before he could see Lily.

He would have liked to see the Turtle. For a moment Catell forgot he was a hunted man and started to figure what to take to the Turtle during visiting hours tomorrow. That's probably what they were waiting for. There were probably men watching the Turtle the way an angler concentrates on his hook, after a long day without a nibble.

Catell leaned against a wall and closed his eyes. Everything started to spin. He walked up and down the street like a very busy man, late for an appointment, or perhaps anxious to get there ahead of time, this being a really hot deal. It didn't work. He couldn't have cared less. He watched a young dish walk by, her high-heeled strut making highlights dance all over her. Just for the hell of it, he pushed himself away from the wall, turned toward the girl, and gave her the eye. She looked back so coldly that the whole vision of her turned ugly. But it wouldn't have taken that much to make Catell lose interest. A minute or so later he couldn't remember what she looked like.

Catell looked at his watch and started for his car. Pulling out in a sharp U turn, he drove up to Sunset and joined the traffic toward Beverly Hills. But he didn't start to make any time until he passed the Beverly-Wilshire, where the traffic thinned out a little. Catell had started to smoke the way Topper used to: one cigarette after another and the windows closed. When he got to the Pink Shell, his pack was empty.

Lily still used the same dressing room where Catell had found her that first time. He went in and waited for her, folding and refolding the empty cigarette pack.

When she came in, Catell got up and smiled. "You're looking good, baby. How was it?"

"O.K., I guess. You been waiting long, Tony?"

She went behind the screen to take off the red corset and net stockings she was wearing.

"Why're you going behind that thing?"

"Just because."

"Because what?"

"I don't know. Just because, you know."

"Come on out."

"Aw, Tony, please. That's not right."

He didn't answer her. He sat with his elbows on his knees, cracking his knuckles.

"How was it, Lily?"

"Reach me that bra, hon. How was what?"

"Where you came from, just now. That party."

"O.K., I guess. We just danced. I sang a song."

"What else?"

"Nothing, Tony, honest. Just a private party and we entertained. You know."

"I bet you entertained. Anybody make a pass at you?"

"Tony!"

"Listen, I know those parties. Did anybody—"

"Nobody did nothing, hon, really. To me, anyway."

"What?"

"Well, some of the girls stayed, you know. They're still there. But nobody tried anything with me. They all know I'm your girl, Tony."

She came out from behind the screen, wearing the white dress, high and smooth around her ripe body, the dress she had worn the first time he'd heard her sing.

Catell got up and took her waist. "They knew you were my girl, huh?"

"They did, hon. That makes me special," and she smiled up at him. "You feeling better now, Tony?"

"Sure. And all this is going to change. One more week, Lily, two weeks at the most, and you and I beat it out of here. No more of this life, Lily." He kissed her hard and she gave the kiss back, slowly, earnestly.

"My number's up, Tony. You sit out front?"

"Don't say your number's up. Bad luck." He chucked her under the chin. "Say, 'I'm going on stage,' or something."

"O.K., Tony. You'll be out front?"

"I'll be right there with you."

They did the number about the evil baron again, and Lily did her song. Catell sat and waited. His throat felt hot and raw from smoking, so he drank a glass of milk. When Lily was through she came to the table and sat down.

"Why don't we go home?" Catell said. He had one hand on Lily's arm, working his palm against her wrist.

"One more number, Tony. The short one. Can I have a drink?"

"Sure. What?"

"Just bar whisky. And a glass of water."

"Bar whisky! How can you stand that stuff? We can afford better, you know. Besides, it's on the house."

"Just bar whisky. I like a little shot. It makes me warm inside. You know, Tony, I don't care for the flavors, I just like the heat inside."

"Of course you know how fattening it is."

"It is?"

"Oh, yes, very, and you are getting fat. Here."

"Tony! The people!"

"And here."

"To-nee!"

"True. At your age, getting fat is a bad thing."

"Tony Catell, you do that once more and I'll leave."

"You'll leave! Where to?"

"I don't know yet, and besides, I wouldn't tell you, anyway. So there!"

They looked at each other and laughed, not really knowing why. And in the middle of their being together, a cold anger suddenly pulled Catell's face into an ugly mask. He got up.

"What in hell do you want?"

"Why, lovin' cup, you old boozer, where have you been keeping yourself?"

Selma came up to the table with a rush, gesturing, looking back and forth between Catell and the seated girl.

"You gonna ask me to sit down, lovin' cup?" She sat down next to Lily.

"This is my friend Lily. And this is Selma."

Selma's wide mouth was spread in a stiff grin and she kept crinkling her eyes as if she was suppressing a real killer of a joke.

"If you knew just how happy this makes me, to see good old Tony again. I've been asking around and around, ever since I got here, Tony, and finding out all kinds of things about you. I hadn't heard about you, though," Selma said, looking Lily up and down.

"I bet," Catell said. He waved to the bartender.

"Me too, lovin' cup. Scotch." Selma looked at Catell as if he and she were the only people at the table. She put her chin in her hands and moved one shoulder. The strap of her evening dress slid down.

"Your thing slid down, Miss—Mrs.—"

"Just Selma, dear. Just call me Selma."

There was an ugly scratch in Selma's voice when she talked to Lily. Lily looked as she always did.

While they were waiting for the drinks, there was a moment of silence, the kind of silence that everybody hopes no one will break, but somebody has to.

Then Selma laughed. "Well, Tony, tell me about yourself. You been doing any good? Uh, pardon me, dear, I don't mean you." Selma gave Lily an indulgent smile.

"Selma." Catell's voice pressed out with a hiss. "Selma, I want you to get one thing straight. Leave the kid alone. In fact, leave her out completely. She's done nothing to you, and you, sister, mean nothing to me. So get off my back, Selma. Just stay off my back."

Before there was an answer the drinks came and Selma lifted her glass. Then she put the glass down without putting it to her lips.

"Don't get me wrong, Tony dear." She kept her eyes down. "I don't mind what you did with the chippie. Now that you and me are back together again." Then she tossed down the drink.

Lily was watching Catell with a puzzled look. His hands were shaking. She stretched her hand out, slowly, trying to touch Catell. Selma turned on her with hate in her eyes.

"Don't you try and wheedle him, you slut. And don't you forget for a minute that your kind—"

That's when Catell hit her.

He did it so fast that nobody saw it clearly, and there was nothing to show for it but a slow red welt on Selma's cheek.

She stared at him open-mouthed. Lily, eyes wide, had

started to get up when Selma's expression changed. With a soft, tired voice she said, "Don't be upset, dear. He's like that. Perhaps you haven't found that out. You would if you stayed with him, Lily. He has crazy ways of getting his kicks. Why, I remember once he woke me up at four in the morning and asked me—"

"Selma, either you stop or you'll regret it for the rest of your life."

There was something in Catell's voice that reached the woman. She swallowed and patted her hair. "Buy me another drink, Tony?"

"No. And now you listen to me. All you and I ever were to each other was a dance and a drink and a jump. That's all. I've asked you once to stay off my back. This time I'm telling you. Keep out of our way and nothing will happen to you. Cross me and you'll regret it. So remember what I say and act your age. That's all I've got to say to you, Selma, and I'm not going to say it again." Catell took a deep breath and sat back in his chair. "Now if you still want that drink, I'll get you one."

"Yes, Tony, thanks."

With the unpredictability of a lush, Selma's attitude had turned helpless and soft. When the drink came, she sipped at it, throwing shy glances at Lily and Catell, never raising her head.

"Tony," Lily said, "I'm on. My number's up."

"Don't say that!" His voice was a shout.

"I'm sorry, darling. I mean—"

"I know what you mean. I'm the one that's sorry. Selma, finish your drink. You're leaving too."

"Yes, Tony." Selma got up, trying to move with a contrite grace. She stepped close to Catell and looked at him through her lashes. "Lovin' cup," she said with a voice suddenly hard, "I'm not through with you yet."

She turned and left.

While Lily did her number, Catell sat hunched at the table, stirring the ashes in the ashtray with a dead match. He knew for sure that Selma was not through with him.

Chapter Sixteen

When the sun came up, Catell was still in the mountains. He had pushed the powerful car all night, trying to get to Pasadena early. It was five in the morning, still time to get to Smith's before noon.

Catell opened the thermos on the seat beside him and drank some of the hot black coffee. He put the stopper back in the bottle and lit a cigarette. He was satisfied with the week he'd spent at the resort.

The place was isolated, with only one telephone line coming in through the long stretch of woods. There were two roads out of the place, one road going downhill to join the main highway, the other going uphill to join the same highway farther away. Then there was one more way of getting out: across the lake, two miles through the woods, and then a different highway that never actually got near the resort. Catell liked the layout.

Inside the main building of the resort there were three major safes, it seemed. There was one for guest deposits, behind the registration desk. Another one, for the hotel intake, was in the manager's office, right off the main lobby. The third safe was a movable, compact job, probably a new model, and it stood in the basement of the lodge. That was the building where the big dance was held on Saturdays, and where the gaming tables operated. The lodge stood close by the lake, and the basement of the lodge was right next to the boathouse.

Catell had the plans in his pocket.

He had stayed at the resort long enough to cover two weekends. He had gambled freely, always dropping a game after a short time, going from one table to another. He had a fair idea what the house took in. On Monday mornings, he figured, there was close to a hundred thousand in that safe in the basement.

Catell had the figures in his pocket.

There was a routine about the way each employee worked. Some were important to Catell, others weren't. He had clocked the ones that were important for over a week.

Catell had the schedules in his pocket.

Nine o'clock. The highway was dipping steadily, twisting through the last hills before the valley of the big city. Catell stopped for gas once and then pushed on. The traffic got thicker, and dusty olive trees lined the long highway that cut through flat vineyards and hot stucco towns.

Ten o'clock. Catell entered Pasadena and found his cutoff. He wound through still little streets that looked alternately like futuristic movie sets and old Spanish settlements. Catell was glad to be almost there. The job he had set up looked good, but best of all, this thing would be over soon. First the cash for his job, then the cash for the gold—waiting in the dust near a desert town—and then he and Lily. They were going away. Mexico? Uruguay? He had a friend in Uruguay. A friend with a business that was legit, as far as anyone could tell.

Catell found the address. He stopped the car under a long port and walked to the front of the house. There were no other cars in sight.

A houseboy opened the door and let him in. It was cool inside. The modern sweep of the building had been deceptive, because there didn't seem to be more than five or six rooms. Catell was led to the rear terrace, where he saw that the house was all glass on one side.

"Mr. Smith will be with you shortly," the servant said.

Catell sat and waited.

When he heard footsteps again, it was a woman. She was a stately figure, gray-haired, and with the graciousness of those who can afford to concentrate on nothing but the pursuit of a well-mannered life.

"I am Mrs. Smith," she said, smiling. "My husband told me he was expecting one of his associates. Please sit down."

"Catell is my name." He sat down again, awkwardly.

"I think I'll ask Kimoto to bring us something cool. Gin and tonic?"

"Fine, that would be fine."

When the drinks were brought, Catell waited for Mrs. Smith to take her glass before picking up his own. The stuff was good. The whole setup was good, he thought. A respectable address, the best little house a man could want, a real lady for a wife. Everything neat, comfortable, and right. The life. How would Lily look when she was older? She wasn't so tall, like Mrs. Smith. Lily was different, too, in the way she acted. Not so polite. But Lily was friendlier; she was quiet most of the time, but really friendly.

"Have you been with my husband long, Mr. Catell?"

"Ah, no, not very long. Just a little while."

"I don't suppose that's unusual, though. In my husband's business, old employees of long standing, so to speak, aren't so essential as they are in some types of enterprise."

What in hell was she talking about?

"But then, of course, my husband has so many business interests. Which one are you associated with, Mr. Catell?"

"Uh, that's hard to say. What I mean is, we're just discussing things. You know, to see what can be done."

"I think I understand." She laughed. "In the investment field you can't always put a precise name to the nature of any given business at hand."

Didn't she know a damn thing?

"Mr. Catell, would you like a fresh drink?"

He accepted another one and they talked about the heat and the lawn.

Eleven o'clock. When she rose, Catell got up too, and she offered her hand.

"I'm sorry my husband is keeping you so long, and now I must run too. I'm taking a little trip and my packing isn't half done. You will excuse me?"

Probably a little trip to Hawaii or someplace. Catell finished his drink. He was getting annoyed with the rising heat and the long wait. He tilted his glass and sucked on the small piece of ice that was left. Then he heard a car crunch on the gravel, and a few minutes later Smith came through one of the glass doors.

"Sorry to keep you waiting, Catell. Didn't really expect you till later. Christ, the heat!" Smith sat down, mopping his big face. "I see you've tried to cool off. Join me in another one?"

"Sure."

"Who's been drinking with you? My wife?"

"We chatted a while. She's packing."

"Still packing? What did you talk about?"

"Investment business."

"Oh."

Kimoto brought two more drinks and Smith leaned back with a sigh.

"How'd it go at the resort?"

"Fine. I got everything here in my pocket."

"Not now, Catell. Let me catch my breath."

"Should be a cinch, that place."

They drank quietly for a while.

"Get your expenses down?" Smith asked.

"Yeah, right here."

"Never mind. How much?"

"Twelve hundred. The gambling—"

"Never mind. Here."

Smith counted out some bills and pushed them across the glass-topped table.

"Not a bad business, this, huh, Catell?"

"Thanks, it's O.K."

"What do you think the take will be?"

"Perhaps close to a hundred grand."

Smith took a cigar out, unwrapped it, lit it.

"Not a bad business, huh?"

"Looks that way."

"Catell, listen. You still going through with your plans?"

"What do you mean?"

"Look. This heist is worth three, four times as much as that gold of yours. Did you ever think of sticking around? Right now, I'm giving you peanuts for your work, sure. But—"

"You trying to pull out from under?"

"I've told you once before, Catell, I don't operate that way. What I'm offering you is a chance to come into my organization."

"No deal."

"What's the matter with you, you crazy nut? Just what's so much more important about heisting a stick of gold for a guy like Schumacher than to do the same work for more dough in this outfit?"

"A hell of a difference, Smith. Forget it. Besides, I got other plans."

"Well, my offer stands. For a while longer. Think about it. Now let's finish up and get going. I asked you to come here so you could give me a lift to Burbank. It's on your way."

They got up and walked to the carport. Catell was gritting his teeth at the delay, but he didn't say anything.

"You drive." Smith sat in the back.

When they pulled up to the side of the machine shop, the heat had become like a simmering liquid.

One o'clock.

There were four other men in the office, none of whom Catell knew. They were waiting in their shirt sleeves, collars open, hair sticky. The air-conditioning had broken down.

"Fellows, I want you to meet Tony Catell, head man on this job. Catell, this is Penny, Gus, Plotke, and Corvean. All good men. They'll go with you."

"I only need three."

"Why?"

"I only need three, Smith. You'll see why."

"Never mind. Gus, you beat it."

"Wait a minute," Catell said. "Why Gus? Maybe I want Gus and not one of the others."

"I said Gus goes." Smith sat down. "All right, gather around. Any time you're ready, Catell."

Three o'clock.

They went over the job for the hundredth time. Every detail, every eventuality, every movement and step.

Five o'clock.

"Plotke, go out there and tell that slob foreman to get some more fans in here. And sandwiches."

"How about some beer, boss?"

"No beer. You drink water till we're through."

Seven o'clock.

"All right, we'll go over it once more. We leave both cars…"

Eight o'clock.

"Everybody here same time tomorrow. And don't write anything down in the meantime. Memorize, memorize."

When Catell drove to Santa Monica he was exhausted. The heat, the tension before the job, his strange faintness, all made him wish for a cool, still darkness and peace.

He stopped at a drive-in on the other side of Hollywood and dialed the apartment. Lily didn't answer. He dialed the number again and let the phone ring a long time. Lily must have gone to the store. She didn't work tonight. Buying some more cans at the store, probably.

Ten o'clock.

When Catell put the key into the door, it opened. Lily came at him in a rush, throwing her arms around his neck, kissing him.

"Hold me, Tony. You've been so long. Tony, Tony!"

Then Catell saw Selma.

She was sitting in an easy chair by the empty fireplace. The bottle on the small table next to her was more than half empty, and she had crossed her legs, swinging one foot against the andiron on the left of the fireplace. Her foot went tap, tap against the sharp spike of the black metal.

"Where'n hell you been, lovin' cup?"

Catell swung the door shut and stepped into the room.

"Tony, make her go. She's sat there for hours, Tony, saying things, drinking, and the phone rang and she wouldn't let me answer, drinking there, talking— Tony, please!"

Catell held the girl close, stroking her back, his head deep in her hair. When Lily stopped sobbing she stepped back and looked up at Catell. He smiled at her, then turned his eyes to Selma.

"What have you been doing to her, Selma?" Catell sounded like ice.

"The facts of life, lovin' cup. I just been tellin' her the facts of life. Right, dearie?"

Lily retreated to the back of the room, pulling her dressing gown around her tightly.

"Anything you got to say, say to me." Catell stepped close to Selma's chair.

"But I got nothin' to say to you, lovin' cup. I was talkin' to the chippie there. She's the one needed talkin' to. You, lovin' cup, got all the answers, so I don't need to say nothin' to you."

"What answers?"

"About us. You sendin' for me and us takin' up again. You shoulda told her sooner, lovin' cup."

Catell looked over at Lily and their eyes met. Catell knew he didn't have to explain. Then he turned back to Selma.

"You aren't making a ripple around here, so why don't you give up and beat it? Why don't you take your booze and your filthy tongue and that vicious mind of yours and beat it, Selma?"

Catell hardly expected her to move, but he had the

wild hope that she might. His insides were crawling with a shivering sickness and there was a pounding in his ears.

Selma didn't move. "Don't try to bluff the poor kid," she said. "I explained everything." Selma picked up the bottle and poured herself another drink.

"Out, Selma."

He stood, staring down at her. She looked up at him over the raised glass, understanding nothing.

"Out!"

"Out," Selma said, flinging her arms back and forth. "Out, out, out, out." Then she burst into a shrill giggling.

"Selma!"

She didn't hear him.

"Selma, shut up!" He reached for her arms, yanking her out of her seat so that her head flopped back.

"Out, out, out," she giggled.

"Shut up, shut up!" He shook her back and forth as if he were possessed.

Suddenly she stopped giggling. Her eyes opened wide, and long folds grew down the sides of her mouth. Before she could start to cry Catell slapped her hard on the cheek.

"Do you hear me, Selma?" His face, sharp and drawn, was close to hers.

With a sudden softening of her face she leaned up against Catell and tried to kiss him.

"You crazy lush!" he yelled, and pushed her back into the chair. There was hate in his motions. "You goddamn crazy lush, don't you know when you're through? You make me crawl, you hear? You make me crawl!"

He stood over her, panting, a wild fevered glitter in his eyes, shaking all over.

"Tony, please!" Lily came forward. "Let her go."

"Tony, please." Selma was mimicking the girl's voice. "Let her go, Tony."

Catell had started to shake from head to foot. He sat down, panting, doubled over.

Selma looked puzzled only for a short moment; then she jumped up and ran to him. Lily was there already. She was stroking his head, murmuring to him.

When Catell straightened up his face was quiet, except for the muscle that jumped in his cheek. Then he got up and turned to Selma. What she saw in his eyes wasn't good.

"Tony," she said, "I'm sorry about everything. Really I am, Tony. Look at me. All I want is to have you back, like before, and me taking good care of you. You need a woman, Tony, not a kid like that."

"Selma, there's nothing to talk about."

"Not a kid, Tony. I'm not saying she's no good, I can tell by looking. But she's a kid, Tony, and you're a man old enough—"

"Selma!"

"Tony, look at us." Selma's voice was getting faster, more urgent. "I'm your kind. Anything you want, I can give you. I can—"

"Selma, I'm sick of your voice."

"Listen to me, Tony. She's no good for you. Look what she's done to you, and look at her. Just a brat. A brat decked out like a woman. Christ, Tony, don't you see. She's nothing but a free lay. I know her kind. She's—"

"Enough, now!"

"—flashy, dolled up, no good. Look at her, Tony. That dumb face, and—and—why, she's got breasts twice the size of mine! It's indecent, Tony. She oughta be—"

That's when he hit her the second time.

She fell. When she jumped up from the floor, her big teeth were bared as if she were going to bite.

"Now you've done it, big shot." She was hoarse. "I told you I wasn't through and you can bet your last dime this is the straight stuff. You think you can get away with just about anything, huh? Well, I've got a surprise for you. And you know who that surprise is? The name wouldn't mean a thing to you, but it's Herron."

Selma was panting now, the words stumbling out, making a mean, clattering sound.

"No, lovin' cup, I'm not talking about a boyfriend. This is bigger than you, big shot. This guy is the FBI. You hear me? The FBI!"

Nobody moved when Selma stopped for breath, and before Catell had got the full punch of her words, she started again.

"And he's a friend of mine, lovin' cup, a real good friend of mine. So you better listen to what I say and do what I say, because one little word, lovin' cup, one little word outa my sweet lips, and you can kiss the world goodbye!"

The hate that shook him was bigger than the world. It tore at his muscles, pushed through his veins with a roar, and he felt as if his skin were too small for him. Without a sound, like a snake striking, he was at Selma's throat, shaking her, crashing her head against the mantel of the fireplace, tasting the blood where his teeth sank into his lip. At first, through the brilliant curtain of his rage, he heard nothing, saw nothing but the ugly face that blurred in front of him. Then he heard Lily's voice, crying with a desperate pleading, "Don't do it, don't, Tony, please! We can leave her, Tony! Darling, I'm here, here!"

And he stopped.

The strength of his feeling was still with him, but it no longer had anything to do with Selma.

"Get dressed, Lily. Fast." He turned the girl around and pushed her toward the door of their bedroom. Trying to follow her, he felt hands clawing at his leg.

"Let go. Damn you, let go!" He was trying to pick himself loose when Selma suddenly released his leg. She rolled back, staggered to her feet. With grotesque movements she lurched toward Catell. Her hair straggled over the contorted face, lipstick a wild smear. One shoe had come off and she limped.

"Let go?" she screeched. "Let go? Let go?"

"Not again, please!" Lily threw herself between Catell and Selma, who was reaching out with crooked nails.

"Let go?" she screeched again. "Let go?" And her nails dug into the soft shoulders of the girl. Before Catell could leap at the crazed woman, she had spun Lily around and tossed her to one side. Lily staggered back, over the shoe, and then there was a curious sound.

Gathering all his rage into the whip of his arm, Catell swung out, but the coiled thing inside him never landed, never exploded.

Lily was on the floor, face up, and yet she was not on the floor. As if suspended in space, her body angled up, gently, toward the side of the dark fireplace. Beneath her neck, where her head tilted, stood the black andiron with the spike.

There was only a slight short twisting, then the soft slump of final surrender to death.

In the first instant of seeing, of knowing, Catell heard the terrible sounds of everything that breaks, bursts, and rips apart beyond repair, and the mad turning of all that moves, speeds, dashes about for a while, turning like a giant wheel, around, around. Then the wheel stopped.

At his side was Lily, still strangely suspended, lax now, and as always her eyes looked out in their quiet, wide way. Catell reached for her hand, then let it drop. The wheel had stopped.

Selma crept forward, staring at the two things there on the floor. "Tony," she said.

There was no answer.

She noticed how the curtains moved in the wind, never quite making it before they collapsed again. It was hot in the apartment.

Eleven o'clock.

When she could not stand the silence any longer, she looked for her bottle. It stood where it had always stood, on a small table beside Catell. She took it, brushing up against his back.

There was some ice in the kitchen, and Selma suddenly decided she needed ice in her drink. When she came back into the room with the fireplace, Catell was still in the same place. And the other one.

"Tony," she said.

When there was no answer, she tilted the glass and drained it.

"You need a drink, Tony."

She splashed whisky into her glass and held it down. She moved it closer, touching the rim to his mouth.

That was the first time Catell moved. He moved sideways, avoiding the glass. That was all.

"Tony, for chrissakes. You know I'm sorry, Tony. You know that, don't you? What do you want me to say? I know this is terrible. Tony, hey!"

She poured the rest of the whisky into the glass.

"Hey?"

Catell didn't answer.

"There isn't anything you can do. Or anybody, hey? This is terrible, lovin' cup, I really mean it. But you're making it worse. Don't make it worse. Listen to me. Listen to Selma, lovin' cup!"

She drank the last of the whisky. Standing in the middle of the room, she looked around. Her shoe was under the leg of the girl. Selma went over and pulled it out. She put the shoe on and poked Catell with her foot.

"You better get up now, Tony. I said— Hey, Tony, what's the matter with you? Get up now. Hey, Tony, I know exactly what we'll do, listen. First we get outa here and head back for Detroit. I been doing you some good there, Tony, really I have. Listen to this. We go back there, and Paar—you know Paar—he promised— Tony, now cut this out! You don't like what I'm saying? Listen, you, Selma is the little girl what can help you, Tony. You and me got a lot of life left, you know? Tony, get up from there, for chrissakes. You trying to drive me bats? I'm not used to talking to myself. You better buck up now, Tony, up, up, up."

Taking him under the arms, she pulled Catell off the floor. He stood without protest. He turned around, facing her.

"Tony, come on now. Now's the time, Tony. Let's blow outa—"

She stopped, wondering at his eyes. He was looking at her, but not really looking. Fumbling in his pocket, he pulled out a cigarette, stuck it in his mouth, lit it.

"That's it, Tony, the old get-up-and-go. Yessirree."

He was still looking her way, but his face was unnatural. Like dead clay, even his eyes.

She smiled at him, cocking her head. Then she stepped around him with a prance, hands on hips.

"Tony boy, hey, Tony boy. Damnit, Tony, say something when a lady speaks to you. Tony boy, you have to forget all about all this here. You and me gotta start out now. I said let's go, you sonofabitch, hear? Christ, where's that bottle? Empty. Chrisalmighty. The cops'll get you, lovin' cup. The coppers! They'll get you, and dead to rights this time. Answer me, you filthy crud, you! The coppers, I'll call 'em, ya hear? I'm calling them!"

Screaming the words, she ran to the phone and dialed. Catell smoked and watched her. He watched her through the whole conversation.

"So there!" She hissed the words in his face. "So there, I've done it, you no-good sonofabitch. The cops are coming and I don't care! I'm sick of you, sick of you!"

Her voice, shrill and hysterical, sank to a blur. She stepped back under his cold stare, puzzled.

"They're coming," she repeated.

"They're coming," he said.

Didn't he care? Was this the end? She started to laugh.

"Little Selma keeps her word, you bastard, even if you don't. Washed up, Catell, and now you know it. You shoulda known before but now you know it. A no-good, washed-up has-been."

Stepping close to him, she grabbed his lapels and tore at them with each word. "Has-been, has-been—"

Time was running out.

"You rat, you! Trying to ruin everything, aren't you? Catell, listen to me. Where's the gold? Open your mouth just once, before everything's over. Where is it, you rat? The gold, where—"

For a moment Catell came alive.

"Say it, Tony, say it. We can still—"

With a wooden motion he reached out and pushed Selma aside. As she stumbled she saw him move away, like an automaton, his back to her, walking to the door. He wasn't waiting for her, and in her haste to follow him she fell again, her hand touching a cold leg. Hysteria ripped at her throat and her scream was like a knife.

Catell was gone when they got there.

Twelve o'clock.

Chapter Seventeen

"He won't get away, you know that."

Driving with one hand and fiddling with the dials of the short-wave set with the other, the detective gave Herron a short look and then turned his attention back to the traffic.

"I don't know any such thing," Herron said.

"Jackie, a guy like this Catell never gets away with anything. History proves it."

"That's the first I heard of it," Herron said.

"Christ, we got the whole town roped off for that bird."

"Sure. He was gone who knows how long by the time we got to that apartment, and it took another half hour to get an intelligible answer out of that howling dervish."

"Whirling dervish."

"Howling. This one was howling. And then you got to figure another hour, a good hour, before your roadblocks would be anywhere near effective. But here's the clincher, Rosen: It's now twelve hours later and we haven't got him yet. History be damned."

"That's only twelve hours—"

"Which you can add to all the time I've already spent missing that hood. Rosen, I am in fact getting the eerie feeling there is no such guy."

Rosen made a sharp turn to avoid a hot rod coming the other way. Traffic was getting worse as they entered the downtown area of Los Angeles.

"Listen, Jackie, that was no ghost what knocked off that one we found on the floor."

"What makes you think Catell did it? Could have been that howling lush there, that Selma dame."

"I don't think so," Rosen said. "I don't think so at all."

They drove in silence for a while. The air that blew in through the open windows felt gritty and hot.

"I think you're wrong, Rosen. I think it was that Selma dame. That is, not counting the chance it was one of those weird accidents."

"Crap," Rosen said. After a while: "Wanna know why I say it was Catell? Because of his record. He's a longtime heavy, he's ruthless and vicious, he never showed any feeling for anybody yet who got in his way, his whole history proves it."

"You know a hell of a lot for never having run into the guy."

"I know crooks, Jackie. But I shouldn't brag. What makes this so simple is the circumstances of the crime. Here he was, laying this young thing, when in walked his moll. Now this young one was probably just a one-night stand, picked her up at that Pink Shell, but this don't cut no ice with that other dame. They all start screaming, and Catell gets annoyed. I can just see him get mad there. But all this time his real sympathies are, of course, with his old-time sweetheart, see? When the one-night stand gets the drift, she starts getting vicious. You know how those little blonde spitfires can be. And that's when Catell has too much. He grabs this dish, the young one, and throws her back into— onto—anyway, you saw it. Now the other one starts to howl. Catell has enough of her too, it looks like, being a woman hater deep down anyway, and starts slapping her around, right? She won't stop, so he just ups and walks out. He's the real filth, and this proves it."

"Christ," Herron said. "You live too close to Hollywood."

Rosen turned into the police garage. "Anyway, that's how I feel about it. And also it might be true, Jackie, it might be true."

Rosen had parked the car and they went upstairs. The inside of the police station was cool. Herron kept moving his shoulder blades to keep the wet shirt from sticking to his back, but it didn't help. He took off his jacket and pulled at the shirt with his fingers. They went into one of the offices and sat down.

"I'll see what's new," Rosen said, and he called the switchboard.

Herron took his hat off, fanning himself. His moist hair started to itch and he rubbed his head. He knew that when his hair was wet or sticky, the balding scalp showed up more. Self-consciously he put the hat back on.

"Nothing," Rosen said, putting the phone down. "They should have another interview out of that Selma." Herron lit a cigarette.

"Interview! You shoulda been there when we tried to question that dame. Interview!"

The door opened and a policeman with shirt sleeves rolled up came in. He was carrying a folder.

"Infirmary sent this over. For you, Herron." He threw the folder on the desk and went out.

"Infirmary?" Herron started to open the folder.

"Probably another *interview*. That's where we took your friend Selma. The state she was in—"

"She sick or something?"

"All I know is they were sedating her when we left. What's it say?"

Herron leafed through the papers in the folder and pulled out one of the sheets.

"Here's a tentative medical report: '...alcoholic, hallucinatory. Severe hysterical state makes diagnosis difficult at present.' Then something here—hallucinosis."

"That's the d.t.'s, the heeby-jeebies."

"No. Not hallucinosis. It's worse."

"Crap. Probably she just needs a drink."

Without answering, Herron went through the rest of the papers.

"Here it says 'Interview' and today's date. This morning." Herron read on. "What kind of an interview! Listen to this, Rosen: 'Q: Did you push the victim? A: Dash. Q: Did Catell push the girl? A: Dash. Q. Was he trying to assault the girl? A: Dash. Q: Was the girl known to you? A: Dash.' What in hell are all these dashes for? What kind of a—"

"They probably mean: 'She screams.' "

"So at least let 'em put that down instead of those crazy— Wait, here's a note: 'Where answer is followed by dash, witness screamed.' "

Rosen laughed, slapping himself on the thigh. "Witness screamed. Boy, that's hot. She's a witness!"

"So shut up already. She was there, wasn't she?"

"That makes her a witness? Christ. She was probably witnessing bats, snakes, and elephants, all waltzing along the molding on top of the room."

"Wait, here are some answers. She says: 'So he came down the long chimney, all covered with snow and the loveliest kind of horsehair—' What the hell?"

"Go on, Jackie, go on. This is interesting."

"Rosen, will you be serious a minute?"

"So go on. There he was and here she was. What happened next?"

"Nothing. She stops. There's another dash."

"Scream, no doubt."

"Rosen, do you know how important that Selma is in

all this? Besides, I don't think it's so funny, all this she's going through. Anyway, here's more: 'I tried to tell him I loved him but the slimy sonofabitch just turned around and out he goes. I love him, I tell ya. Jeesis, I want him around. Come back, Jackie—come back, Otto—come back—' Then she goes on with all kinds of names. Wait. Jackie Herron! She's got my name in here too!"

"I told ya, Jackie. All she needs is a drink."

"Why don't you shut up?"

Herron started to flutter the pages irritably, trying to find one sane clue in that demented interview,

"Here, wait. She gives places: 'Santa Monica, Manitou, Toulouse, Louse, House, Grouse—' Off again, I guess." Herron put the papers down and leaned back. "Guess we gotta do our own figuring."

"Any notion where he's heading?"

"No. South, probably."

"To get his gold or just to get away?"

"Both, I guess. It's probably the same to him."

Southeast of the city a shivering man sat crouched behind the wheel of a big car, roaring over the hot highway, and thinking of nothing. He just drove. With the dull, single-minded determination of an animal he held out against the terrible weakness that liquefied his bones and made his muscles like dead meat. He was thinking of nothing, but he drove toward the desert.

"Anything come in during the last three hours?" Herron stood behind the man at the short-wave set. The monotonous garble of police calls and report messages filled the room, but none of it interested Herron, because none of it told him anything about Tony Catell.

"Hold it, Mr. Herron, here's something now." The

man scribbled notes, then took his earphones off. "Man answering description of Catell gassed up at this cross-road here. Take a look at the map. Looks like he's going to Palm Springs, maybe? He had a stained bandage on one hand."

"This sounds like it. Relay that. I'm going to take a cruiser up there."

Rosen drove with Herron. They kept the short-wave on but nothing new came on.

"Bet that murdering bum is plenty scared by now." Rosen turned the siren on to get himself a clear way through the traffic. "If he's really in that neck of the woods, he must have slipped two of our checkpoints. How in hell he did it, I don't know."

"You underestimate those types, Rosen. When they want something, they're driven by furies, and nothing gets in their way."

Catell knew he was close to the place but it meant nothing to him, except that he was close to the place. Not any more. His awareness of things was automatic, and his actions merely coasted on the strength of what had been planned long in the past. So he looked as though he were coming from somewhere and going somewhere, but since he had left the apartment, far back sometime in Santa Monica, there had been no will in him. The wheel had stopped turning.

"You know what's going to happen if that bird ever leaves the highway, don't ya?" Rosen said.

"What? We lose him?"

"That's right. We lose him."

"Catell's a city boy, don't forget. He wouldn't hole up

out there someplace. He wouldn't know what to do."

"Where there's a will, there's a way."

"My guess is he isn't going to stop for anything. He needs distance, Rosen. He's trying to get away as fast and as far as possible. And not just from us. From the mess he left, too."

Rosen and Herron were on the highway now, traveling at a good clip toward the darkening east.

"Think they'll snag him before dark, Rosen?"

"Ought to. Look at the map. Blocked here, here, here. Even this burg here, Joiner's Creek, they even got an alert out for him there."

"Not that it matters," Herron said "If I know my city boys, they'll always stick to the highway and rely on a fast car. And Catell's no different."

The rutted side road wound through a landscape of caked dirt and dry sage. Every so often there were rocks. Catell never slowed down. He had started with high speed; he had stayed with it. He did what he was doing because he was doing it.

When the road dipped he saw the green trees for a moment. They were some distance off, but they meant that Joiner's Creek was there. Catell slowed down, looking. With a sudden twist he pulled the car off the road, bumped over the sage that rattled under the car, and stopped beside a gray outcropping of rock.

Catell got out of the car and walked around the rock to a place where the stone sank vertically into the ground. Squinting in the failing light, Catell stooped low, walking, then stopped. He went to his knees.

For a faint moment the old fire tried to leap in him again, but there was no fuel to feed it, and it died.

Catell just dug.

When his nails hit the metal, he reached down, felt the handle, and pulled out the dented cartridge box. He carried it to the car and set it on the floor in the back. Then he drove away.

Herron had slept badly and the morning sun coming up over the flat land felt like a sledgehammer. He left the cabin and walked across the gravel court to the diner. Rosen was already there, working on a cheeseburger and French fries.

"Sit down, Jackie, sit down. Ready for some breakfast?"

"Rosen, please, you trying to make me sick? And keep those potatoes out from under my nose."

"Jeeze, you always like this in the morning?"

"I forgot my toothbrush. I thought this chase would be over before long, so like a fool I took off minus a toothbrush. Coffee, miss. Black."

"Don't bother buying one, Jackie. This caper is almost up. We got the planes out now. Patrol just came by and told me."

"You talked the same way yesterday, Rosen. By now history is beginning to prove you're wrong."

"Crap. How can we miss? You know what this country-side looks like from up there? A pancake. Like a pock-marked pancake."

"For chrissakes, Rosen, let me enjoy my coffee. And put those damn potatoes someplace else."

"Sensitive, ain't ya? Well, Jackie, I can understand that. Some guys, when they don't have their toothbrush in the morning—"

"Aw, shut up."

After they had drunk their coffee, Rosen pulled out a map.

"Take a look here, Jackie. We figure he's in here, and bottled up good. Now the planes are going to spot this area there, other side of Joiner's Creek, and over here, too. I can see that crazy hood right now, shivering behind some rock there and watching the planes overhead."

That same afternoon the big car was racing its sharp shadow down the white highway. Catell handled the car with no wasted motion. He sat stolidly, without blinking, even though he headed south with the sun in his eyes most of the time. Sometimes he switched on the radio and listened to the police calls. But you couldn't tell by looking at him that he knew they were chasing him farther north; he had crashed the dragnet during the night.

During the day he stopped twice. Once he stopped for gas, and the other time for water. He forgot to eat. Toward evening the heat got worse and he passed truck after truck loaded with melons, lettuce, and more melons. The Imperial Valley. The dragnet was far behind. When Catell saw the sign that said Brawley, he took the next road to the right. He avoided big towns and traffic with a sure habit, catching the main highway again on the other side.

That's when he blew the tire. The car took a wild lurch and threw Catell sharply against the side of the door. He grabbed for the wheel, fighting it while the car bumped to a halt on the soft shoulder of the road. He got out and changed the tire. It took him only a short time, but when he straightened up from the wheel, he suddenly felt deathly tired. Waves of fuzzy blackness came and passed; his eyes burned with a purple ache. He had to lean against the car and wait for his strength to come back. Then he went back behind the wheel and started the car. The wheel with the shredded tire was left behind. It lay near the edge of the road, forgotten. Or perhaps Catell just hadn't cared.

He should have.

In the middle of the night, two trucks loaded with produce came barreling down the road. They piled up on top
of each other, spraying fruit and leaves, because the lead
truck had hit the discarded wheel. From the time that the
state troopers checked the scene to the time when they
knew that Catell was nearby, only a few hours had passed.
They checked the odd-sized tire; they wondered about the
wheel; then they took a routine rundown of cars wanted,
and they found that a man who had slipped them in Los
Angeles was driving a car like the one that had lost the
wheel.

"Did you hear that?" Rosen said, turning down the short-
wave.

"No, I didn't hear that. I was musing to the soft hum of
the tires on the shiny road. I have no other interests in
mind, so I don't listen to the radio."

"Now, Jackie, don't act like it was my fault. Didn't we
do everything there was to be done?"

"Obviously, no."

"Well, it beats me how he got out. We had every crossing
sealed up, the planes—"

"Yeah. And now I'll tell you how he did it. He left the
road and went straight across the prairie, as big as life and
as long as he pleased."

"But the planes—"

"At night, my friend, they couldn't tell one shadow
from another, even if they had been flying. And all Catell
needed to get around was a little moonlight. Now, where I
come from we got ditches next to the highway. You couldn't
just barrel off the road and into the prairie, even if we had
prairie."

"Don't think we won't keep that in mind from now on. Besides, there's no prairie in the Imperial Valley. We got him bottled up but good this time. Just let him try hiding in a lettuce field. There's only one way out for him now, Jackie, and that's straight up. Or straight down, maybe."

And Catell began to notice it.

He began to notice how the cars were bunching up in front of him. They were coming fast and at even intervals from the other direction, but his side of the road had become slow and glutted with cars.

Roadblock.

He couldn't see it yet, but that didn't mean a thing; there were twists in the road. Creeping more slowly all the time, Catell edged forward, hoping for a side road before the roadblock came in sight. There weren't any, just fields and fields with plants standing low and in straight rows as far as the horizon. His hands started to sweat. Closer, slowly closer.

He had almost passed it before he saw the dirt lane that angled off through the fields. It was a wide, rutted road, used only by the trucks that picked up the produce from the fields.

With a sharp swing Catell jerked the car out of his line, across the highway, and into the field. Everybody could see him, but he didn't worry about it. In a cloud of dust he raced along the planted rows, which seemed to come at him like a spreading net.

There were no turns, no dips. When the end of the field came in sight, Catell noticed that the next highway was empty. He turned onto the pavement, letting the car leap forward on the smooth cement. A curve, and there they were again. Two cars across the road, two guys putting up a striped wood barrier, a third one hitching at his pants, just looking. When they saw the black car tearing around the bend they straightened up and looked. The one who had been hitching his pants up started to wave at Catell in a halfhearted way before he jumped. The other two men were already in the ditch. When the barriers flew up in splinters and Catell watched his left front fender crumple like a piece of paper, a couple of shots cracked out from behind. They didn't hit a thing, because when the car was clear of the roadblock Catell pushed the gas pedal to the floor and shot off like a rocket.

But now he wasn't just driving anymore. Part of his sharpness had returned, tingling through his body like a charge of electricity. Long before he heard the sirens howling after him he was looking for a way to leave the highway, to ditch the car, even to make a lone stand, no matter what.

Because nobody was going to get Tony Catell.

When the clump of woods showed up on the left, Catell slowed down enough to take a screeching turn off the road. He kept the car on the narrow lane that wound through the trees, but his attention was wandering. Sirens wailed, sometimes loud, sometimes barely audible. He was trying to figure their position, their direction, but the wooded road, winding to avoid a tree, a rock, kept throwing off his judgment. When the sirens got louder Catell had to slow down. The powerful motor was barely growling and the car dipped and swung, edging ahead, nodding its hood.

Catell started to jump at movements in the trees, started to jerk the wheel too hard. His slippery hands itched, and that faint trembling began to shake him again.

Then the sirens stopped.

They must be off the highway. Where were they? The unbearable tension ripped loose in Catell and he jammed his foot down against the floorboard. The car shot ahead with a howl, barely missing a tree. For a few seconds the straining car found its way, and then, just as Catell could see the trees thinning out in the distance, the tons of roaring power shot off the road into the crunching underbrush. For one strangling second the car kept edging along, wheels whining; then the motor choked.

Catell didn't get out right away. He sat limp, smelling the strong odor of gasoline, breathing with a shallow movement. When he got up it was with the same dull automatism that had wrapped him for most of the trip. He got out of the car, listened, and reached into the back for the cartridge case. The weight of the thing made the handle slip out of his fingers and he had to lift it with both hands. Carrying the box in his arms, he started to jog toward the thinning trees.

The light was almost gone. The cloying night air smelled of earth and rotting matter, but Catell didn't notice. The short distance through the woods had drained him of all strength and he could barely get his breath. Through his swimming vision he saw a light in the distance. It was steady and small, looking like all the distant lights that call to children lost in the woods.

Catell started toward the light. He stumbled and lurched across the ruts of a field, his eyes on the light and nothing else. It seemed as if hours had passed when he saw what it was. There was a farmyard and a truck, and two men were standing by the motor, their heads under the hood. Every so often the motor roared, and then they jiggled something under the hood.

Catell crept forward, the box a heavy weight in his arms.

No one saw him, heard him. Not many farms in the Imperial Valley have animals. When Catell got to the back of the truck he smelled the load. Stacked high over the panels, lay a soggy mess of wilting lettuce leaves and rotting stalks.

First Catell threw his box up, then he climbed after it. When the truck pulled out of the farmyard, Catell was buried in the soft mush of decaying stuff. It was warm, soft, and vibrating quietly with the motion of the truck. Catell almost went to sleep. Or perhaps he did. What made him jump was the sudden change in speed as the truck slowed down, crawling along the road with gears whining. Catell knew what it was without looking.

Roadblock.

Struggling as if in a morass, he came erect, the box with the gold under his arm. There were lights ahead, and without any thought but to get away, Catell jumped. Dragged down by the weight of the gold, he hit the pavement with a bad jolt, rolling sideways and into the ditch. He lay there feeling nothing but pain and terrible exhaustion. When he looked up, he could see five cars, all in a line, and the checkpoint. He could have yelled at them and they would probably have heard.

With the last twitching of his muscles he clawed himself slowly up the side of the ditch into the meager bushes that marked the end of another field. More lettuce, he thought, and then a thick unconsciousness dropped on him like a weight.

When the sharp sun hit his face he bolted up with a panic that knew no degrees. There was the road, here the field, his hand was on the battered box heavy on the ground. The road was empty and even the checkpoint looked deserted in the sun. The barricades were farther than he had thought. And there was no one in sight.

Hefting his box, Catell got up and turned toward the field.

"Hey!"

They were there, two of them, by the barricade. "Hey, you!"

Catell turned the other way, down the highway.

They were there.

As in a bad dream, they had popped from nowhere, coming toward him. Catell started to run across the field.

"Hey, Mack, stop!"

For a second the old anger rose in him, giving strength to his flight, but then there wasn't enough. All he could do was run, the box dragging on his arms. The box? My gold, he thought. This is my gold.

With a sullen stubbornness he made his feet thump along the narrow rut. They were behind him, yelling sometimes, but he didn't have the strength to turn. Even the fear had left him. In front of Catell the lettuce field stretched to the horizon. The long vanishing lines of the field converged as in a nightmare, gathering him forward as if in a rush of speed, but never changing, never making the horizon come. The sky was wide and naked, the field lay in a shadowless sprawl, there was nothing but the nightmare lines leading nowhere.

Catell's legs pounded the sod with monotony. He didn't know whether they were coming; he didn't consider whether they were coming. Trapped in an expanse of nothingness he went forward, forward, and when the horizon changed it was like a sudden shock to him.

Sloping down the field, he hit a row of trees and bushes that grew along the edge of a creek. On the other side was another thicket and beyond that a field. But Catell didn't look that far. When he plunged into the narrow under-brush they came across the rise behind him, but Catell didn't think about that, either. Gasping painfully, he stum-bled on, looking only for the densest, darkest place in the nightmare of his flight.

Where the low creek had broken the soft bank, Catell crawled under an overhang of roots and earth. Dragging the heavy box along the ground, he squeezed and bur-rowed into the recessed space, like a night animal seeking the shelter of the dark. Then he just lay still. He listened to the roaring in his ears, the hard beat of his straining heart, and he could also hear the soft sifting of the earth that ran down from above, gently. He fingered the box absently while his dull eyes looked along the creek. A little farther down he could see the battered form of an old house, black in the brash sun, and on the side of the house a large old water wheel that had not turned in a long time.

The little stream, the sun filtering through the leaves, the old wheel of the mill in the light—it was a romantic scene that lay before Catell.

Then his ears caught the voices and the rustling. They were here. Catell heard it but didn't move, except to push his heels into the earth to lean closer into the damp, close hole he had found. Catell was tired. He lay there looking, and he never thought that they might get him. When the voices had passed above him he moved once, to shift his weight. After a while his idling fingers touched the box at his side. Turning his eyes to see his gold, Catell undid the latch. The box toppled, lid open.

He looked for his gold but saw nothing. There was no strength in him to turn the box and shake it out. Catell leaned forward, looking, and the sun brought out a quick white gleam deep in the box. It crossed his mind that the gleam should be yellow, a warm gold yellow, but his thought was without interest and he let it pass. Then he pushed the box out of the way to rest himself more closely against the covering earth.

He did not look at the gold again. It sat inside, in the dark hole where it had lived out its rottenness, with only a lost speck of mercury to show what had happened. It was clean gold again.

Once more Catell moved. It was then that the new ache spread through his chest, and he had to raise his head to get breath. It suddenly gripped his chest with a hellish pain, ripping at his heart and freezing the motion of his chest.

That too passed, and Catell sat quietly a while longer.

When they found him the sun was in his open eyes and they were staring at the wheel that had stopped turning a long time ago.

THE
END

Get Hard Case Crime by Mail...
And Save 50%!